LINE CHANGE

BRITTNEY MULLINER

D1518453

UTAH FURY HOCKEY BOOK THREE

This is a work of fiction. Names, characters, organizations, places, events, and incidents are either products of the author's imagination or are used fictitiously.

❀ Created with Vellum

ALSO BY BRITTNEY MULLINER

ROMANCE:

Utah Fury Hockey

Puck Drop (Reese and Chloe)

Match Penalty (Erik and Madeline)

Line Change (Noah and Colby)

Attaching Zone (Wyatt and Kendall)

Young Adult:

Begin Again

Live Again

Love Again (Coming Soon)

Charmed Series

Finding My Charming

Finding My Truth (Coming Soon)

Standalones

The Invisibles

For exclusive content and the most up to date news, sign up for
Brittney's Reader's club here

LINE CHANGE

Rule 205 (b)
Players may be changed at any time during play from
the players' bench, provided that the player or players
leaving the ice shall always be at the players' bench and out
of the play before any change is made.

(per USA Hockey Rulebook,
https://www.usahockeyrulebook.com/)

1

NOAH

This had to be a dream. It couldn't really be happening. I was going to wake up any second in my shared room in a grungy apartment.

Now.

I pinched myself. No, seriously. This couldn't be my life.

"This one is yours."

The plaque over the locker read N. Malkin. Holy crap. This was real. The Utah Fury locker room was state of the art. Decked out in black and red to show off the team colors with the logo in the center of the floor.

My jersey, skates, and helmet were waiting for me. Number forty-one. Malkin.

I touched the jersey. The cold fabric slid through my fingers as I turned to look around. This was better than I imagined.

When I was drafted last year to the Utah Fury, I thought that was the greatest moment of my life. But being put on their farm team in Boise wasn't the dream I thought it would be. It was a lot of grueling practices, traveling in buses, and very little pay.

Playing in the AHL was a stepping stone to my dream, and I was here. I was in the locker room with Coach Rust. There was a jersey with my name on it. My dream was coming true.

He gestured to my locker. "Set down your bag and I'll give you the full tour."

I was trying to remain calm, like I saw the inside of my dream team's lair on a daily basis. Soon I would.

This was unreal.

I wanted to ask where the guys were. I couldn't wait to meet them. Especially Wyatt Hartman. He was one of my idols. Even if he was only five years older than me. I'd been watching him for years, and now I was going to be playing with him.

Hopefully. I probably wouldn't be on his line, but maybe we'd crossover.

If this dream could come true, so could that one. I wasn't far from it.

Coach Rust led me through the equipment rooms, small meeting room, large theater room, training room, gym, and hydrotherapy area. He gave me a little speech as we were walking, explaining things to me, but I was in sensory overload. I took it all in like I was seeing Disneyland for the first time. As a kid. Because it wouldn't be as cool now.

Who was I kidding? Yes, it would.

I'd never been. One of the downsides of being Canadian and playing hockey since I was three. Not much time for vacations or normal kid experiences.

Not that I minded. I was playing in the NHL now.

Disneyland would always be there.

My chance in the major league would not.

Rust turned to me looking much calmer than I felt. Of course, this was all normal to him. He was here every day. I wondered if he had felt this way the first time he got here. Probably not. He'd been a star on the Dallas team back when he was a player. He was probably used to it by the time he got here. Part of me never wanted to get used to it. I wanted to appreciate where I was and all I'd accomplished every time I entered the arena.

I wouldn't become a jaded player who took this for granted. I wouldn't get caught up in the fame or money or politics. I'd seen too many amazing players get caught up in it. Just a few years ago, the number one draft pick, Randy Hall, lost his contract within six months for taking a sponsorship he shouldn't have. He cared more about the money than the opportunity to play in the NHL.

I'd met my childhood hero after a game when I was around eight. He blew off the fans and told us he wasn't going to sign autographs. He said he wasn't paid to do that. I'd decided that day, if I ever made it I would appreciate each second and give back to the people that supported me.

It had been my dream to play professionally since I could remember, and I would not screw this up like those guys had.

Rust stopped and faced me. "Do you have any questions?"

I shook my head. When I called my parents last night to tell them I was finally moving up to the majors they gave me several pieces of advice. They said to be agreeable. Be easy to work with. Be teachable. Do not cause drama. Do not make them regret their decision.

I took each word to heart. They had helped me get this far, they obviously knew what they were talking about.

"No, sir." I said. "I appreciate you taking the time to show me around."

He nodded once. "Let's go meet with Coach Romney."

I closed my eyes and drew in a deep breath. Here it was.

I followed him through the maze of rooms until we came to his door. I took another deep breath and relaxed my shoulders before I walked in.

I'd met him briefly at the draft and I'd seen him on TV, but being in his office, alone, was intimidating.

I sat down and wiped my palms on my pants.

"It's good to see you Noah." He smiled but it didn't reach his eyes. Why did I feel like I was in trouble? I couldn't have possibly done anything to upset him yet. Maybe he saw something from a previous game he didn't like.

"You too, sir."

"We're glad to have you here. I do wish it was under different circumstances."

I cringed a little. I felt horrible that it took Howe getting seriously injured for me to move up to the team, but I wasn't going to let it get in the way of my performance.

"Coach Rust and I want to make sure you feel welcome on the team and make sure you are taken care of. We know the transition from the AHL to the NHL can be a bit overwhelming."

I tried to think of what he meant but couldn't guess. Maybe it was the bigger stage?

"I've spoken with your agent and advised that he set you up with an assistant and financial advisor."

Oh. He didn't think I could handle the fame and money that came with the major leagues. I refrained from telling him my parents raised me right.

"He said he would set something up," Coach Romney said.

"Thank you, sir."

"Good. Practice starts in twenty, so go get ready. I'll see you on the ice."

I stood and shook his hand before leaving the office. Coach Rust had disappeared, so I figured I was finally on my own. Good thing I remembered the tour well enough to get back. Asking for directions on my first day would be embarrassing.

I walked into the locker room and went back to my name plaque. A few guys were milling around, but they ignored me. I wanted to take out my phone and send a picture of my locker to my parents, but I didn't want them to think I was lame. I was a rookie, but I didn't need to make a show of it.

"Hey, Malkin."

I turned to see Wyatt Hartman walking toward me with Erik Schultz and Reese Murray at his side. *Don't pass out. Don't pass out.*

"Hi, Mr. Hartman. Captain. Sir."

I wanted to punch myself in the face.

He smirked. "Hartman or Wyatt is fine."

I nodded like he was my commanding officer.

"Welcome to the Fury. We took a look at your footage from the farm team, and you're pretty good. We're glad to have you here."

He watched me play? Deep breath. "Thank you, Hartman."

Schultz eyed me. "Get changed, your first real practice is about to start."

I looked at them and realized they were already dressed. I needed to hurry, or I was going to be last out. Drawing negative attention is not something I wanted on my first day.

"Thanks. I'll see you guys out there."

I changed and wondered what Schultz meant about my first real practice. I'd been playing since I was three. I think I knew what to expect.

5

About thirty minutes into the drills I understood.

I'd never known my legs could burn like this. If I were able to walk tomorrow it would be a miracle, and we still had two hours left.

A whistle blew, and the guys gathered at the bench for water. I didn't want to sit, knowing I'd never stand again so I grabbed a bottle and moved in small circles.

"How are you doing?" Reese Murray was leaning against the board, casually sipping away like he wasn't about to die. How nice.

"I'm okay."

I could hear the fatigue in my voice, and judging by his smirk, so could he.

"It'll get easier. Don't push yourself too hard the first few days. It's better to be slow now, then sitting on the bench by the end of the week."

He was right. I needed to pace myself. I needed to prove myself, but I wouldn't do that if I was passed out on the ice.

"Thanks."

He nodded. "We were all where you are at one point. We understand and so do the coaches. The AHL is no joke, but you're playing with the championship team now. They didn't get there by taking it easy."

As if I'd forgotten that little detail.

"Was it a change for you?" I asked. "Coming from Boston?"

He smiled. "Yeah, but I caught up fast."

Good. I wasn't the only one. I knew I could do it. I would be able to keep up soon. Hopefully within a few days. There was a reason these guys were the very best in the world. They didn't slack off. Ever.

The whistle blew away and the guys dropped their bottles. My thighs cried as I skated back to the center.

Coach Rust separated us, and we played four on four games for the last hour. It was crazy to watch my heroes play each other. They laughed and joked as they raced past me, and when it was my line's turn to get on, it was an out of body experience.

I was defending for Olli Letang! The greatest goalie in the league. Schultz and Hartman were coming toward me looking like they were in on a secret.

I got ready and was able to block Schultz, but he passed to Murray and Olli had to catch it.

Brassard gave me a pat on the shoulder as he passed me. It was a tiny sign of acceptance. I'd held my own. I'd managed to do what I was supposed to. I looked around, but no one was paying attention to me. At least I wasn't getting negative attention. No disappointed looks or shaking heads.

I moved back to the center where they were dropping the puck and took my position. My side won possession, so I faded toward the back, watching, anticipating where I would be needed.

Hartman took the puck and shot it toward me. I turned and raced after it, passing to the corner. It got picked up by Porter and he took it back to the neutral zone. My heart was racing like I'd run a half-marathon in record breaking time. This was what I'd lived for the past seventeen years. Sure, these guys were insanely good, but when it came down to it, this was the same sport I'd been playing last week in Boise. I knew how to play my position and I was good at it.

That realization sunk in and I began to enjoy myself. I was at the top of my career, and this was just the beginning.

Hartman changed direction and came charging toward me. I braced myself, ready to predict his move. His eyes darted to the left, toward the goal. I took a step that direction, just in time for him to dodge to the right.

He scored, and it was my fault.

I looked around as he and Murray talked. Brassard skated by, no pat. No fist bump.

I'd made a mistake. I fell for the misdirection.

No one said anything to me, but I could feel it. The eyes on me. The wondering if I have what it takes.

It wouldn't be the last time. I knew I'd have many more slipups, but this one stung.

The rest of practice got harder by the minute. I was in my head. I knew I needed to shake it off, but doubt was setting in.

2

COLBY

My phone vibrated on my desk and I considered ignoring it until I realized it was Bryce Parker calling. I muted my music and answered.

"This is Colby Wells." I used my most professional voice.

"Colby, it's Bryce. How are you?"

I pretended like I was on a first name basis with him. "I'm doing well, Bryce. How are you?"

"Well, I need some help and you were the first person I thought of."

Liar. There was no way I was even on his radar.

"What can I help you with?"

"I have a client." A professional athlete of some sort. Bryce was an agent, but I didn't know who he represented. "He just got called up to the NHL and I think he may be in over his head."

That wasn't uncommon. Young kids get drafted, get a big signing check, spend it all, and end up filing for bankruptcy by the time they're twenty-three.

"Sounds interesting."

"He's a good kid, just young." Probably some fresh-faced

nineteen-year-old out on his own for the first time. "He's just moved from Boise to Salt Lake."

"Well, he's nearby."

Bryce laughed like I'd just told the best joke. I was simply stating a fact. I'd graduated from the University of Utah last year and had enough connections here to keep me employed.

"He's only been down here for a day. He's in a hotel."

I looked around my home office. Okay, that was being generous. It was my living room that I'd put my desk in and decorated with sports memorabilia from my grandpa's collection.

He'd left everything to my dad and me. I had signed baseballs from all the greats, and posters from every major sport. Working with these great men and women had been my goal since I was a little girl. Unfortunately, I lacked the coordination to be a decent athlete, and I wasn't cut throat enough to be an agent, so I'd turned to being a personal assistant. One of my college roommates went on to work for the Utah Jazz and connected me with one of the players looking for part-time help. Since then I'd worked for a few of the basketball and soccer players from the area, but a hockey player would be new.

I'd met Bryce at an event a few years ago. I was there with one of my soccer players and Bryce confused me for a cocktail waitress. It had been embarrassing but I'd made an impression. We say hello when we run into each other, but this was the first time he'd ever called me.

"So, he needs someone to set him up here?"

"Yeah, and you know the area. I was thinking you could get him settled in."

"Sure." For the right price. Not that I was in a position to negotiate. Impressing Bryce could establish myself as an assistant and lock in future jobs.

"I spoke with his coaches and we agree he needs someone full-time. I'm not sure for how long, but at least the next two to three months."

A full-time client who lived close by, handed to me on a silver platter? Yes, please.

"Let me take a look at my current workload and see if I can fit in another client at this time."

"Of course. Just try to get back to me by the end of the day."

"Thank you. I'll talk to you soon, Bryce."

"Bye."

I hung up and nearly threw my phone. I'd managed to play it cool, but this was an amazing opportunity! Bryce has a decent client list and owns his own agency with over fifty athletes. If I pulled this off, I would be set.

No more part-time stints or one-month contracts. I might even be able to get a bigger apartment. One with an actual room for my office. One in a slightly better part of town.

I eyed the stack of envelopes on my desk.

Student loans. I was drowning in them. Taking a client with Bryce could get me out of the hold.

I could be a dedicated personal assistant. Manage everything. My degree in accounting might actually come in handy. I'd wanted to break into this world, so I could be the man behind the curtain for some of my generations greatest. Rub elbows with my heroes.

One phone call and I was a gigantic step closer.

I knew those endless events and galas would pay off eventually! I stood up and did a mini victory dance before getting back to work. I really did have other clients I needed to focus on. A full-time assistant position was more than a nine to five job. I'd be on call at all times. Sure, there would be down time where I could work on other things, but I needed to see how much I could handle.

Realistically, though. I'd drop some of my part-time work before turning down Bryce.

I went through my calendar and emails. Things have been pretty light lately. One contract would end next week, so I'd have even more time. So, only three clients would be left. I managed social media for one of them, managed a calendar for another, and the last one had me run weekly errands. That was the only one that could get tricky, but I would manage. If I had to pass it off to another PA, I would.

I could do this.

After sending out an email to my social media client about his upcoming posts for the week, I called Bryce back. I didn't want to come across as overeager or that I was too available. I was in demand. I had things I needed to move around. He couldn't just call me and expect me to drop everything.

I laughed to myself while I waited for him to pick up. I could tell myself those things until I finally believed them, but I would give up everything to work with Bryce.

"Bryce Parker."

"Hi Bryce, it's Colby. I was able to move things around, so I'm available."

"That's what I like to hear. I'll send you the contract and NDA now."

We hung up after I gave him my email address and I stared at my screen, refreshing my inbox until it came through. We didn't discuss money. I had a feeling Bryce assumed if you were talking to him you knew he was worth the big bucks.

Finally, a new message alert popped up and I clicked on it while holding my breath.

I read his short message and opened the attachment.

I scanned the page until I saw it. This was for three months? Three months of work and I would make more than I've made in the past two years...combined.

This had to be a mistake.

But it wasn't. This was life in the real world of professional sports.

I could do this. I could do anything for seventy thousand dollars.

I read through the rest of the terms and shrieked. If I made it through the next three months and got a positive review from the client, Bryce would send me more referrals. I'd be able to build my own clientele list. I could build a business of people working with me.

This could be life changing.

I signed the contract and other paperwork and had it sent back within ten minutes. A minute later I got a response with my new client's name, address, and his bank. There would be a credit card waiting for me within the hour.

That was important because my first task would be finding him an apartment. He couldn't live in a hotel for very long. I double checked that everything I needed to get done today was finished and made sure I didn't have any new emails before grabbing my purse and heading out.

I headed to the bank first. Everything I needed to do would require money and having access to my client's card was perfect. I wasn't sure how they could get me a card so quickly, but I knew better than to question Bryce. I'm sure the bank was used to requests like this from him.

All I had to do was show my ID to the teller and she

handed me a thick, metal card. I didn't want to know what the limit was. Not yet. I wanted to play pretend for a little bit, but on my way out a banker called my name.

I turned to the tall, middle aged man and smiled. "Yes?"

"I'm Jon. Mr. Parker called and asked me to give you a brief run through of Mr. Malkin's accounts. We'll add you as a signer as well."

I nodded and took a seat across from him. Bryce worked fast. I was added to a few of my other client's accounts, but this was by far the fastest it's happened.

"Mr. Malkin has a checking, savings, and investments account. We will be managing the investments."

I nodded but would want to look at that later. I may not have met Mr. Malkin yet, but he was my client and I wanted to make sure he was in the best position possible. Hockey players were high risk and I wanted him to be set in case any accidents arose.

"His signing bonus was deposited this morning. Mr. Parker had us put it into his savings with the plan to put down money for a rental. Mr. Malkin knows how much he was paid, but we don't want him spending too much of it."

I nodded. I was glad they all seemed to have his best interest in mind. I didn't want him to be one of those tragic stories of someone who had it all and lost it.

"He will also have monthly deposits made by the team, but Mr. Parker recommended that at least half of that be split for savings and investments."

He slid a paper across the table to me with Mr. Malkin's monthly salary.

Holy smokes.

Most of my other clients were in this range, but they were older. More established. This guy was a kid.

"Thank you, Jon. I'll keep that in mind as I get him set up."

I signed a few papers to have me added to the accounts. Mr. Malkin's signature was already on them. How? Did he sign them electronically? There was no way he beat me here.

"If you ever have any questions, please don't hesitate to call."

I took the card he offered me and left. Once I was in my car, I let the reality of my situation wash over me. This was a bigger deal than I could have expected. I was in charge of so much. So much responsibility. And trust. How did Mr. Malkin feel about a complete stranger managing things for him? Picking out his apartment? Getting him a car?

Would he want to have a say?

Some people wouldn't care. They'd just be grateful things were being taken care of. Others would want to be a part of the decision-making process.

There was only one way to find out. I needed to meet this mystery person.

I sent him a text introducing myself and asked him to let me know when we could meet. In the meantime, I sent out an email to a few of my contacts about available apartments. He didn't need anything super fancy, but being close to the arena would be important.

My phone started ringing and Noah Malkin's name filled the screen.

"Hello, Mr. Malkin." I hoped I sounded professional and confident, but I was nervous. This was the first time I'd gotten a job without meeting the client. What if he didn't like me?

Why wouldn't he? I would do a great job, be available as he needed and otherwise stay out of the way.

"Just call me Noah." His laugh made him sound young, but his voice was smooth and deep.

"Right, Noah. I'm just leaving the bank and Bryce told me an apartment was your first priority. I was just wondering if you would like to meet and go over your preferences or if you would like to come with me."

There was noise in the background. Lots of voices. "I'm actually pretty busy right now. Could you find a few options and I'll see them tonight?"

"Sure, did you have any specific things you'd like?"

"Maybe a second bedroom in case someone comes to visit."

I waited, surely that couldn't be it.

"Anything else?"

"Not really. Nothing too girly would be nice."

Huh. This was either going to be super easy, or he'd see the options and suddenly have way more opinions.

"Sounds good, Noah. I'll have a few options for you to see after dinner."

"Thanks, I should be done by seven."

"Perfect, bye."

I hung up and blew out a breath. That had gone better than I expected. I really hoped he was as low-key as he sounded.

My phone buzzed with a new email. An apartment building with an opening. I checked the address and it was just down the street from the arena. Perfect. I needed to get there and check it out before it disappeared. The housing market was crazy, and most units were gone within the same day.

3

NOAH

Colby texted me an address and asked me to meet her there after I was done with dinner with the team. They took me to a pizza place and a few of their wives and girlfriends showed up. It was crazy to hang out with them. Like I was their equal. I guess maybe I was, but it still didn't seem real.

I put the address into my phone and got to the apartment building about ten minutes later. It was close to the arena and had a park across the street. It seemed nice, but I didn't want to get too excited. It looked expensive.

"Good evening." The doorman greeted me and pulled the door open for me.

"Hello."

I walked past him and into the modern black and white lobby. I expected a check-in desk and restaurant, like a hotel, but there was a small sitting area in front of several elevator doors.

A woman walked up toward me. She looked about my age, wearing a cream coat over jeans and boots. Her honey brown hair was long, almost to her waist. When Bryce had told me my new assistant's name was Colby, I thought she was a he. When I'd talked to her on the phone I'd figured it out, but seeing her was definitely a shock. I hadn't expected her to be so... hot.

"Hi, I'm Colby Wells." She extended her hand and I made a conscious attempt to not stare.

"Hi, I'm Noah."

Her smile lit up her face. She was the kind of person who smiled with her whole body. Her shoulders relaxed, and her face softened. I'd been worried she was going to be the serious type with her leather briefcase and fancy clothes, but when she smiled she opened up.

"Great, I have the key if you want to go see the unit."

I nodded and followed dumbly behind.

Once we were in the elevator she pushed the number six button. "I've seen three units today. We can see the others after this if you'd like."

"Okay." I sounded lame, but I didn't know what else to say. I'd lived with guys from the team in Boise and before that I was in sponsors' homes while I was playing in the major juniors. This was my first place.

"This is a two bedroom, two and a half bath unit. Both bedrooms are suites with their own bathrooms, as it's nice to have a separate one for guests."

"Oh yeah. That is nice." As if I'll ever have guests over. Hopefully, I'll make some friends, but that wasn't a guarantee.

The elevator door opened, and she led me down the hall. She unlocked the door and stepped in. The lights were already on, revealing a large living room and kitchen. There wasn't a dining room, but I doubted I'd need one. I looked around at the furniture. I sat on the sofa and nodded. Not too bad.

"Is it furnished?" Having to go shopping for a couch and tables and beds sounded terrible.

"Yes, this one is. Everything you see is included."

Sweet. I looked out the window at the view. I could actually see the arena from here. That was pretty awesome.

She showed me around the kitchen and bedrooms, which were larger than I expected. Both had king beds and fancy bathrooms with waterfall showers.

I looked around for a bit while she waited in the living room. It had everything I wanted. A doorman was a nice plus too. Mom would like that. She worried about me living in a city, despite the fact I was six-foot three and over two hundred pounds. I wasn't exactly an easy target.

I went back to the living room where Colby was on her phone. "It's perfect."

She dropped the phone in her bag and smiled at me. "I'm glad you like it."

"Tell me about the other options. Are they the same size?"

"One is a two-bedroom, two bath about five minutes away." She pointed in a direction away from the arena. "The other one is a really cool loft option. It's closer to the school though."

"Are they furnished?"

"Not the loft."

Cross that one off the list. "How about pricing?"

"This one and the other two bedroom are the same, but the other unit doesn't have a pool or doorman."

"Then I'll take this."

Her eyebrows shot up. "Are you sure? You don't want to see the other units?"

I shook my head. "No reason to waste either of our time. This is clearly the best option."

"That's what I thought, too." She smiled like she was hiding something.

"Good."

"So, I put down the deposit and signed the paperwork."

She did? "How?"

She shrugged. "I weighed the options and I knew this was the best for you. Bryce already has me on your accounts, so I put the money down and he signed the contract."

Huh. So, this was what it was like to have 'people'. It felt weird that I hadn't signed the contract myself, but Bryce knew what he was doing better than me. His and Colby's jobs were to make my life easier. They were there to focus on things like this, so I could focus on performing.

"Thanks, Colby."

She smiled and walked to the front door. When she opened it all of my bags were sitting there, waiting. She had this whole thing planned?

"How did you get those?"

"I went to your hotel and packed everything for you."

I didn't know if I should feel violated or relieved. "You're good."

"Thanks." She pulled my bags into the living room and shut the door. "Welcome home, Noah."

I looked around and realized it felt right. "Thank you. I really appreciate it."

She nodded and pulled out a tablet from her bag. "So, the biggest thing is out of the way. What else do you need or want done?"

I sat on the couch and she sat across from me. "I don't have any food here."

She nodded. "I sent you an email with a list. You just need to go through and check the things you like. I assume you have preferences with your protein and supplements so let me know what brands you like, and I'll be sure to get those as well."

I looked at my phone and noticed the email notification. "Wow. Thanks."

She grinned and waited.

Oh. Right. "I know I have a car and all, but it's the same one I bought for myself when I was sixteen."

"I figured that would be something you'd be interested in. I've created a monthly budget taking into consideration your salary, rent, basic expenses, and savings. You can afford a car payment of five hundred dollars."

Whoa. I haven't had a car payment...ever. I'd seen the commercials with how much cars lease for and with a budget like that I could pick nearly whatever I wanted. Well, nothing crazy.

"Do you have a preference of a car, truck, or SUV?"

Did I? I hadn't thought about it. I'd driven my old, beat up sedan without ever thinking about something else. I couldn't ever afford it.

"An SUV would be nice." It would probably be easier to get in and out of.

"Great. I'll take a look around, but don't worry I won't buy anything this time." She winked, and I could feel my cheeks burning.

"After this, I trust you to buy a car."

She grinned and began typing again. "What else?"

I had no idea. Bryce and the coaches were convinced I needed a personal assistant, but I didn't know what to have her do. "What do you normally do?"

"I can manage your social media accounts. Set up a maid or chef if you'd like. Manage your calendar and sync it to your phone. Respond to your fan mail."

"I don't get fan mail."

She looked up and smiled. "Oh, you will."

I wasn't sure about that, but she seemed sure. "I don't think I'll need a maid or a chef, but the other things sound good."

"Okay." She began typing again. "The team handles your travel for games, but if you need any help planning trips let me know."

"Thanks, Colby."

This was a lot to take in but having her here, getting used to her, helped. It was nice knowing I wasn't here alone. She might not necessarily be my friend, yet, but I had someone I could call, someone to talk to.

"That's what I'm here for." I returned her smile, but it was a jab to my stomach. She was here because she worked for me, not because she wanted to. Well, maybe she wanted to be here, but it was because she was getting paid. It had nothing to do with me. How lame was I that I cared that she liked me?

"I think that's it, unless you need me to do anything now? Do you want me to run to the store and get some basics for you?"

It was nearly nine. I hated sending her out, but it would be nice to have some things for the morning.

"Actually, would you mind showing me where the store is?"

"Not at all, let's go."

I hadn't meant that she come with me, but I was selfish. If she was willing, I wanted her to.

I was a grown man, but I was intimidated by doing the simplest things. I'd lived a weirdly sheltered life. People around me had always taken care of things, so all I had to do was play hockey.

My roommates were better about errands, and I'd given them money for groceries, so I could use whatever was in the kitchen. I was on my own now. Well, with Colby. It was like adulthood with training wheels.

She led me down to a parking garage that I'd missed earlier. That made this place just that much better. No scraping off snow in the mornings.

"This way." She unlocked her little SUV and I got in the passenger seat. It wasn't a new model, but the interior was spotless. She took great care of it. It made me trust her even more.

"Do you want a regular store, or a health food store?" She pulled out and waited for my response before turning.

"Just regular for now."

She nodded and explained where we were going, hopefully I'd remember for next time. I could use my phone for directions, but I wanted to get to know my neighborhood.

Even in the store, she was efficient and to the point. We were in and out within fifteen minutes with everything I needed for the next few days. Milk, yogurt, granola, fruit, coffee, bread, and eggs. She thought of everything as I walked around aimlessly. She made sure to only mention healthy foods, which was good even though I was craving junk food.

I ate clean during the season. Pizza had been pushing it tonight. I'd be eating salads and grilled chicken for the next few days to balance it out.

When we got back to my building I stopped her from getting out. She'd done enough for me. I could bring up a few grocery bags on my own.

"Thanks for everything you did today, Colby."

She smiled and adorable lines appeared by her eyes. "No

problem, Noah. It was nice meeting you. I'll update your calendar tonight and start looking for an SUV."

"Have a good night."

I shut the door and waved as she pulled away. Once in the elevator I pulled out my keys and stared at the newest one. My first place. I couldn't wait to show my parents.

I got off on the sixth floor and turned right. That's when I realized I hadn't been paying attention. I had no idea what number mine was. Was it the third door on the left? Or the fourth? I didn't want to just start trying doors. What if the person was home and called the police? I couldn't call Colby. That would be humiliating. She would think I needed a full-time babysitter.

I stared at each door trying to remember. Six-seventeen or six-nineteen?

They were exactly the same. Nothing to differentiate them.

I was just going to have to try. I slid the key into the closest door as carefully as I could, making no noise. It went in and I was able to turn it. Yes! First try. I was six-nineteen.

First major moment. Walking into my first home with my own groceries. I was really doing this.

Luckily, I wasn't on my own. Colby was better than I could have imagined. She was sweet, kind, patient, smart, and absolutely beautiful. I'd have to ask Bryce what the dating policy was.

4

COLBY

Noah sent me a text asking me to come to his practice. I wasn't sure what he wanted me to do. Just watch him? I figured he forgot something and asked what he wanted me to bring but he never replied. On my way out the door, I considered asking Bryce, but I didn't want him thinking I was incompetent. Especially on my second day.

I got into my car and ran through a list of possibilities. Skates? Pads? A change of clothes?

All of those could be remedied by the team.

Soap? Shampoo? A favorite post-workout drink?

I'd know him well enough to be able to make these predictions soon, but right now I was flying blind.

Was he hungry? They should have food in the team room. Maybe they didn't have anything he liked. Ugh. I hated this. I was always certain of things with my clients. It was my job to be.

Rather than playing a guessing game, I drove to the arena. Whatever he wanted, I'd get. I'd have someone deliver it if needed. But I needed to know what it was first.

I waved a pass Bryce had sent to my house yesterday at

the security guard. He let me through the gate and into the private parking garage below the arena. I was surprised by the mix. I was expecting rows of luxury cars, but there were only a handful of really ridiculous vehicles. My little SUV wouldn't stick out too much.

I walked toward the elevator and stared at the buttons. Up or down? I had no idea. I picked one and waited. When the doors opened the floors were labeled, thankfully. I selected the main level and came out at the entrances to the portals. I walked to one and realized I was in the very center of the arena, behind the benches. I took the steps, looking for Noah. I wasn't sure of his number and with all the gear all of the players looked the same.

I was halfway down the lower bowl when someone called out. I turned to see a stunning brunette coming toward me. I stopped and waited for her to meet me.

"Hi, I'm looking for Noah Malkin."

Her smile seemed forced. "I'm sorry. This is a closed practice. We don't allow the public to watch, but you can come back on Wednesday from eleven to one."

I shook my head. "I'm not here to watch. I'm Noah's assistant. He texted me to meet him here."

She narrowed her eyes and looked down at the ice. "Come with me."

I followed her as if it was my choice. I had a feeling if I didn't listen to her orders I'd be kicked out. No one had warned me about security inside the arena. Not that this woman looked like security. She was wearing a Fury shirt, though, so who knew.

She stopped above the bench and hit the glass three times. One of the players, number fifty-four, turned around.

The player pulled his helmet off, revealing sweaty blond hair. "What?"

"Where's Malkin?"

I was surprised she referred to him so casually.

He turned and looked around before pointing to the corner of the ice. Noah was trying to hit the puck away from another player and was hit from the side when he wasn't paying attention. I cringed at the impact. That couldn't feel good.

"Give them a minute. They should rotate soon."

I nodded, not taking my eyes off Noah.

"What's your name?"

I glanced at her while she studied me. "Colby Wells."

She stuck out her hand. "Chloe Schultz."

"Nice to meet you." I shook her hand once before looking back at my client.

He was out in front of the goal watching the action taking place in the middle of the ice. I'd have to work on my hockey terminology. I was good with basketball and soccer, but Noah was my first hockey client. I knew the basics, but I needed to step it up.

A whistle blew and everyone on the ice came to the bench as the groups rotated. One of the players stopped in front of Chloe.

"What's up?" He called out looking concerned. It probably wasn't normal to have people hanging out here.

"Get Noah."

He yelled down the line and Noah's head shot up. "What?"

The guy pointed up at us before turning around and watching the game taking place.

Noah moved around the other guys and toward us. "You're here!"

"Yeah, of course. What do you need?"

His smile grew. "I want you to watch me."

27

What? I rushed out here to watch him practice?

Chloe made a noise, but I ignored her. "You want me to watch?"

He nodded. "Yeah, let me know if you see anything I can improve."

With that he turned and sat down on an empty spot on the bench. He couldn't be serious. I wasn't his mom. I didn't have time to sit and watch him play. He wanted my notes on his abilities? Wasn't that what coaches were for? I barely knew the sport, let alone his position.

"Come on, I'll show you where we sit." Chloe tugged my elbow.

I followed behind her still stunned. She led me to the opposite side of the arena where a group of a dozen women were sitting.

"This is the Pride. We're the wives, girlfriends, and family of the players." She turned and faced the group. "Everyone, this is Colby. She's Noah Malkin's assistant."

A few of them waved or said hello. They were probably wondering what I was doing here. Join the club, ladies.

"Come sit down here." Chloe lead me to the front row where a purse and laptop were waiting. She sat down and patted the spot next to her. "I work in the front office, but I come down to watch each practice, so if you're ever here feel free to join us."

I slid into the seat. "Thanks."

"Malkin's new. How long have you been working for him?"

I checked my watch. "About twenty-four hours."

Her jaw dropped but she quickly recovered. "And he's already having you come down to watch? Either he has no idea what to do with you, or he has a little crush."

She winked but I quickly dismissed that. No professional athlete would be interested in me. Not when they have access to models and actresses.

"I think he's just young and feeling a bit insecure."

"How old are you?"

Her question caught me off guard. "Twenty-one."

"How old do you think Noah is?"

He looked young, but he had a baby face. The dimple when he smiled didn't help. He was clean-cut, unlike most of his teammates so that didn't help him look any older.

"Eighteen?"

She laughed. "He's twenty, and his birthday is coming up."

"How do you know?"

"I wrote his bio for the website."

Huh. I really never would have guessed. Knowing he was basically my age changed things. It shouldn't have. He was still my client, but it made me feel less like I was the adult in the situation. More like we were equals.

We were, even before, but now. Now I felt like there was potential. For us to be friends. Just friends. Of course.

"So what else does he have you doing, besides being his personal cheerleader?"

I rolled my eyes while she laughed. This better not be an everyday thing, otherwise I'd have to bring my laptop to work here. Chloe did it, so maybe it wouldn't be that weird.

"I found him an apartment yesterday and took him grocery shopping. I'll also be working on his social media accounts and managing his calendar."

She nodded. "Erik doesn't have an assistant. That's kind of me."

"Erik?"

She laughed. "Sorry I assume everyone knows. Erik

Schultz..." She pointed to a player in the far corner chasing the puck. "... is my brother. We live together."

I nodded but looked down at her finger. She was engaged.

"My fiancé is Reese Murray." She pointed to another player who was waiting in front of the goal.

This girl was connected. No wonder she was the one who approached me. She works for the team, is engaged to a player, and related to another one. I was surprised the mascot wasn't named after her. Who knew, maybe it was?

"That's crazy."

I hadn't meant to say it out loud, but luckily, she just laughed. "It really is."

"So, you work for your brother too?"

"He doesn't pay me, just lets me live rent free. And he bought me a car. But I do most of the work of an assistant, so if you need any help with anything team-related let me know."

I would. She seemed like an invaluable resource. I pulled my phone out of my bag and held it out. "Can I get your number?"

"Sure." She typed quickly and handed it back. "What's your next thing to do?"

"He needs a new car."

She smirked. "Don't let him find out what Erik drives."

His car must be one of the ridiculous ones I saw. "Don't worry. I've already made a budget plan and he's sticking to it."

"Good." She paused for a moment. "If you want help looking, I can come with you."

"Oh no. I'll be fine."

She smiled. "I know you're more than capable, but I

figured you'd want someone who knows a bit about the team to hang around."

She was right. She had information I could use. Plus, she knew the team better than anyone. I could have her help me get up to speed.

"Okay, if you wouldn't mind I'd appreciate it."

"Perfect. We'll go after practice."

Wow. I expected her to say we'll get together in a few days or something. She was like me. Down to business. Get things done. I liked her.

The rest of practice passed quickly. A few of the women came up and introduced themselves as they were leaving, and Chloe stayed by my side.

"Come on, I'll show you where their locker room is and where you can wait for him after games."

She ended up giving me a pretty thorough tour of the tunnels below the audience. She showed me where the coaches' offices were, the training room, the weight room, the theater, and stopped in front of the team locker room.

"I'm sure most of them wouldn't mind if a pretty girl walked in, but I don't want to scar you."

"I appreciate that."

Once guys started streaming out of the doors, she introduced me to them making sure they knew I was with Noah. Maybe she wanted to make sure they didn't think I was a fan girl or someone sneaking in if they saw me around.

"This is Erik." She pulled on the arm of a player, making him stop. He was tall, and built, and oh so handsome. I knew I shouldn't think that about my new friend's brother, but I couldn't help it. "Erik, this is Colby. She's Noah's assistant."

He smiled and offered his hand. "Nice to meet you. Noah's a good kid."

I nodded and watched him walk away. I may have drooled just a tiny bit.

"He got engaged just a few days ago."

Of course, he did. Men who looked like him weren't meant to be single.

"That's nice. Are you two planning a double wedding?" My smile grew when she cringed.

"No way. I've shared enough with him. We'll each have our own days."

Noah finally walked out, looking exhausted. He looked up and noticed us, and a smile broke out exposing that dimple. I needed to tape over it or make him grow a beard or something. He couldn't just flash that at unsuspecting victims.

"Hi Colby." He looked from me to Chloe with a questioning look.

"This is Chloe Schultz."

His eyes lit up. "You're Erik's sister, and Reese's fiancé, right?"

She nodded. "You've heard about me?"

"Yeah, just a bit."

I reached out and touched his arm. "We're heading out to look for some cars. Do you need anything else?"

He seemed to think about it. "I don't think so. Could you look at some Range Rovers? Some of the guys have them and they said they're the best."

I didn't want to embarrass him in front of Chloe, but I also didn't want to get his hopes up. I didn't know if he could afford it.

"I'll see if it would fit in the budget."

His smile dimmed but he nodded. Why did I feel like his mom? We were the same age, but he seemed immature. Not in an annoying way. It was just like he hadn't experienced much. He was ignorant to things. That was a better way to explain it.

Maybe he'd grown up sheltered? That would explain why he didn't have a good grasp on everyday things. Like picking out a brand of cereal last night.

Noah waved and smiled. "Thanks, I'm going to head home."

"See you later." I watched as he walked away. I wasn't staring at his body. Of course not. He was my client. My boss. I was checking to get a better idea of his shirt size. What would it take to cover those biceps? An extra-large? At least.

Chloe grabbed my arm. "Come on, Colby. Let's go shopping."

5

NOAH

After seeing Colby at practice, I realized I probably should have been clearer in my text. I didn't need anything. There wasn't an emergency. I just wanted her to see me play. I wanted her to know I was serious. That I was worth it.

Bryce told me I could have her do whatever I wanted, well, short of harassment. I wanted her to see me play. I wanted to know what she thought about me. As a player, of course.

Was it wrong to want someone there to support me?

When Murray told me about the Pride, I thought Colby would want to join. She could get to know those women so when it was game time she'd have someone to sit with.

Cause she would come to my games, right?

I really didn't know where the lines were. She was being paid to be my assistant, but I didn't need that. I needed a friend.

Maybe that's why I asked her to come. I wanted someone to be there watching me. Cheering for me.

When I saw her outside of the locker room I'd been so

excited. I thought she was there to tell me good job. But she just wanted to know what I needed her to do.

Work.

It was all she did.

I wanted her to break out of that, but I wasn't sure how to get her to do it.

When I walked into my apartment, without having to second guess which door mine was, I went straight for the kitchen. I didn't have much, but I grabbed a bowl and filled it with yogurt and granola.

I fell onto my couch and turned on the TV.

It felt strange to be alone. I had this whole place to myself. No roommates. No teammates barging in. Just me.

It was lonely.

I thought I would like it, but one day alone and I was ready for company.

I should have asked to go with Colby. She probably assumed I had other things going on. Professional athlete things, but Bryce hadn't told me about anything. No new sponsors or ads. No photoshoots. So far no one cared.

Hopefully that would change after my first game tomorrow night. Once people saw me play, they'd be interested.

Hopefully.

Getting some sponsors would be great. It would secure me as an NHL player and bring in some extra income.

I picked up my phone and texted Bryce to let him know I was interested. Not that it wasn't common sense, but maybe some guys didn't like that kind of thing. I did. Well, I would.

My phone buzzed, and I picked it up, surprised he got back to me already. It wasn't him, though. Colby sent me three pictures. A new Jeep, Audi, and a Jaguar. I guess the Range Rover wasn't in budget. I wanted to push for it, but I knew Colby was just being responsible. I should be grateful she was keeping me in check and making sure I didn't overspend, but the other guys had nice cars. I wanted one too.

I texted her back and asked if she test drove them.

She responded right away. She and Chloe agreed on the Audi. That was fine with me.

The phone rang, and I answered it. "Hi Colby."

"What color do you want?"

I hadn't thought about it. My parents bought their cars based off the price. No one in my family had ever bought brand new. I guess this was how the other half lived.

"Um black?"

"Okay. I'll let the salesman know. We'll need your signature on a few documents, but I'll text you and let you know when they're ready, so you don't have to wait around here."

"Oh. Thanks." She hung up and I looked around the room. She must expect me to be super busy. So busy I can't wait at the dealership for my own car. I didn't know what to do with myself.

I should work out, but I was dead from practice. Weight lifting sounded like a nightmare.

My parents were at work, so I couldn't call them.

I flipped through the channels until I found Sports Center. I wasn't really paying attention. Should I text the guys and see what they're doing? Maybe we could hang out?

No. They all had lives. I was probably the only one staring at the wall. Bored.

Just then the TV shut off and all the lights went dark.

What on earth?

I pressed the power button on the controller, but nothing happened. I stood and went to the light switches, but they stayed dark. Had the power gone out? What if the bill didn't get switched over and they turned it off? How long could I last without electricity?

I grabbed my keys and wallet and went into the hall. There were a few emergency lights on, but it was dark there too.

Well, at least it was the whole floor. Maybe the whole building. They'd have it fixed soon.

I took the stairs down, grateful I was only on the sixth floor, and got in my car. I texted Colby asking where she was and started my car. She responded with the name of the dealership, so I typed it into my phone and followed the directions.

She might not expect me there yet, but I should probably see the car I was buying. Maybe sit in it, see if I even like it.

I got there a few minutes later, and saw Chloe and Colby standing just inside the doors. I walked in and they both turned at the same time.

"Hi Noah." I smiled at Chloe but stopped when I saw Colby's look. She didn't look confused. She looked annoyed.

"Hi, Colby. The power went out in the building, so I figured I'd come down and see the car."

"The power went out? Oh, my goodness. I'm so sorry, Noah. I'll call right away." She stormed off, already on her phone.

"I didn't mean for her to try to fix it. I was just telling her why I was here already."

Chloe smirked. "It's her job to make sure your life runs perfectly."

I shrugged. I didn't want that to be her problem. No one could prevent everything.

She leaned toward me. "Do you want to see it?"

It took me a moment to realize what she meant. The car. My car. Right.

"Yeah."

I followed her out of the building to one of the front parking spaces. There she was. An all-black SUV, complete with black wheels and dark tinted windows. "This is nice."

I held my hand up to see inside. The interior was white. The contrast was cool, and I knew I'd appreciate the light leather in the summer.

"It drives really well, too."

"Can we take it out?"

She shrugged. "Sure. I'll go tell the salesman." She left while I continued circling the SUV. It was really nice. Much more luxurious than anything my family had ever owned. We weren't poor by any means, but my parents didn't splurge on things. Not with three kids, especially one with costly hockey lessons and team fees.

I knew they supported me and never held the money against me, but I felt bad owning this before them. They were the ones who deserved a nice house and fancy cars. After all they did for me. All the money and time they spent on me and my career. I owed them the world. And I would give it to them. As soon as I was on the team for good. I would buy them everything I could.

"Here you go." Chloe tossed me the keys and got in the passenger side.

I got in behind the steering wheel and touched the smooth leather seats. "No Colby?"

"No, she's negotiating with the sales manager."

I started the car and smiled as it purred to life. "Why?"

"She wanted to get the price down. She told them you'll be photographed in it a lot, so they'll be getting free publicity. She told them if they came down, you would keep the license plate frame on so people would know where you shopped."

That sounded ridiculous. I laughed but stopped when I saw Chloe's raised eyebrow. "What?"

"You're in a position of power now, Noah. You need to be aware of that. Not only because of what you can get using that power, but the influence you have. You'll be watched. Make sure you're on your best behavior. Not only for yourself and your family, but for the team."

Those were heavy words. I let them sink in as I drove around the block.

She was right. People would start to take notice of me. I didn't want to make a bad name for myself, or the team. I didn't want to give them any reason to kick me off, or not offer me a contract at the end of the season.

I pulled back into the parking spot and got out.

"What did you think?" Chloe asked as we walked back into the dealership.

"I love it."

"Good, cause we're ready to sign." Colby came up from behind us with a wide smile.

"Did you talk them down." Chloe asked with a grin.

"Oh yeah. I had them eating out of my hands. They practically want to give the car away."

Was she being serious? She was really able to negotiate? "Thanks Colby."

She nodded. "Just doing my job. Come on."

I followed her back and signed where I was told. They were taking my old car as a trade in and giving me more than I expected. I was sure that was due to Colby as well.

"You're all set, thanks for coming in Mr. Malkin. We look forward to seeing you play tomorrow."

"Thank you." I felt awkward not knowing the salesman's name, but he didn't seem to mind.

Colby handed me a set of keys and put the other set in her purse. "Just in case you get locked out or need me to move your car."

She didn't need to explain herself. I trusted her.

From the very beginning I had. Which was strange for me. I felt like I was an easygoing, open person. But I had a hard time letting people in. Probably because I moved around so much and was always on new teams. I didn't get to know most people well enough to trust them.

That wasn't the case with Colby. The first time I saw her was enough. Maybe it was her take-charge personality or her stunning looks that she didn't seem to notice. Whatever it was, it got to me.

6

COLBY

My other clients' work was finished for the week, so I was able to focus on Noah. His first game was tonight, and I made sure to let him know I was available all day for whatever he needed. I wasn't expecting any emergencies, but I wanted to help calm his nerves.

"Are you sure I don't need another suit?"

He was standing in his living room turning while looking in a mirror. I shook my head. Again.

"That one looks perfect." I wasn't exaggerating. Noah looked so handsome. It was one thing to see him in his uniform, but there was something about a guy in a suit.

"The guys all wear designer, though. I don't want to look cheap compared to them."

I looked to the ceiling, willing patience. "They all have tailors who custom make their suits, Noah. What you have is fine. Plus, it's not like we could get one fitted for you in the next three hours."

He looked at me through the mirror. "If I were more demanding I'd make you do it just to prove you wrong."

I raised an eyebrow and waited for him to apologize.

He'd been saying things like that all morning and usually realized his mistake minutes later.

"Colby, I'm sorry. Again. I wouldn't do that. I'm just nervous."

"I understand, Noah, but you look great in that suit and it's not going to change how the game goes."

I wanted to lecture him about spending money he didn't have, but I'd been through it with him several times. He saw what the other players had and wanted it. Not that I could blame him. He'd been thrown into a completely different world. He wanted to fit in. Unfortunately, the job of being the voice of reason fell on me.

"Maybe, but I'd feel better going in." He said quietly.

He wasn't going to drop it. If it was in his head that he needed a custom suit to look the part of a professional player, there wasn't anything I could do to talk him out of that idea. I could drop a truth bomb though.

"Noah, your contract with the Fury is only through the end of the season. That means you can't live like the rest of the team. The best thing you can do right now is focus on you, and how well you perform. That's all that matters. You need to work to prove to them that you deserve to be here next year."

Not that I knew that was even a possibility, but it seemed logical. If he proved himself, he could stay. In an ideal world.

He nodded and finally turned his back to the mirror. "Hopefully I get to play."

This was his second focus so far. He kept saying that like it was a possibility. I'd already learned that everyone on the bench plays. The game is too fast-paced for even the best player to stay on the ice for the whole game. He'd get rotated in plenty.

"You need to get that out of your head."

He came closer and sat down next to me. "I just want to get out there. Once the game starts I'll be fine."

"I know you will. You just need to focus on that." I checked my watch. We still had an hour before he needed to leave. "Let's take your mind off it for a bit."

I reached for the remote and scanned through the channels. I was going to go fast through the sports channels, but Noah's hand shot out. "Stop!"

I froze and looked at the screen. It was him. Noah was on the TV.

"Noah Malkin is a fresh face joining the Utah Fury tonight following the devastating injury to their defensemen, Andrew Howe. All eyes will be on him tonight to see if he can live up to the spot he's taking over."

I glanced at him out of the corner of my eye to see his reaction. He was sitting there, slack jawed, staring at the screen.

"That just happened," I said.

He nodded.

The topic changed to basketball and Noah fell back against the couch. That had to be a shock. It wasn't everyday you're being discussed on national TV. People would be watching him and talking about him later. No pressure. I waited for a reaction, but he was practically catatonic.

"Noah?" I poked him, but he remained unmoving. "Buddy?"

He blinked which I accepted as a sign of life. "They said my name."

"Yes, they did."

He blinked again. "They showed my picture."

"They did that as well."

"They're going to be watching me."

43

"Several thousand people are going to be watching. That's kind of the point of professional sports." I tried to inject some levity to the situation. I didn't want him to start freaking out.

Note to self, don't let Noah watch or listen to anything before a game. He would have to sit in an empty room. Alone.

That wouldn't psych him out. Too much.

"Yeah, but they're going to be watching me. Me."

I reached for his arm and patted it. "You've got this, Noah. I've seen you play. You're amazing. Now is your chance to show everyone else."

He turned his head to look at me. "You think I can do this?"

I tried to focus. He was my client. My boss. I had to ignore his baby blue eyes that reminded me of summer days. They were sucking me in. It was like he knew his effect on me. He blinked, and I snapped out of it.

"Yes, I know you can."

"Can we head in yet?"

I checked my watch as if it had been more than ten minutes. "I'm just going to freshen up then we can go."

He looked back to the ceiling, so I took that chance to go. I went to the hall bathroom and closed the door. I was wearing a Fury T-shirt I'd gotten from the fan store at the arena and jeans. I was technically on the clock, but I figured Noah would rather I look like a fan than a business woman. Plus, I was sitting with Chloe and the Pride at the game, and I knew they would be decked out in gear.

I fluffed my hair and applied some lip gloss before walking out. "Ready?"

He jumped up and walked to the door. "Yeah."

I picked up my purse as he grabbed his bag and opened the door, waiting for me.

"Do you want me to drive?" I eyed him on the way down the elevator. He was rubbing his hands together and tapping one foot. It was a short drive, but I wanted to get to the arena in one piece.

"Would you mind?"

"Of course not." I watched him get in on the passenger seat before settling in. As we drove I tried to think of the perfect thing to say. I glanced over at him, but he was staring out the window. He was in his head, and I didn't want to interrupt him. When we got to the arena there were a few fans taking pictures and Noah seemed to sit up when he saw them. He waved, and the crowd returned with cheers.

I pulled in past security and parked. He was grinning widely when we got out of the car.

"That was pretty cool." I nudged him with my elbow.

His smile grew and reached his eyes, making them sparkle. "Yeah it was."

"You've officially arrived, Noah Malkin."

He turned bashful and looked away. "Thanks Colby."

When we got to the elevator I stopped. He needed to go down to the locker room and I needed to go up to the main floor. As much as I wanted to stay with him and tell him everything was going to be just fine, he was on his own now.

"Noah." He turned and looked down at me. It wasn't often we stood next to each other, and it was a reminder of how large he was. At least six inches taller than me and built like a wall. I swallowed. "You're going to do so great today."

He nodded.

"Don't stress. You'll be fine once the game starts."

He smiled briefly. "Thanks."

I didn't know what to do next. Hug him? Pat his shoulder? Tell him to break a leg? "I'll see you after?"

"Yeah."

I pressed the down button for him and stepped aside. When the doors opened he stepped in and held it open for me.

"Let's do this."

I stepped in and we rode down in silence. When the doors opened to the lower levels, Noah walked out. He stopped and looked over his shoulder and smiled before walking away. I felt like I was watching a little baby bird fly from the nest for the first time.

The doors closed, and I flashed my pass to the security guards on the main level. There weren't too many people around yet, but I checked to see if anyone from the Pride was there. We had an hour before game time, and I should probably eat. Even though my stomach was in knots. I didn't want to show it in front of Noah, but I was nervous for him.

This was a big deal. A major night for him. This was his chance at his first impression on the league. He had one chance. I had my fingers crossed that he'd make a good one.

"Colby!" Chloe waved at me from the front row. She was sitting with Emma and Sophia, two of the wives I'd met at practice.

I took the stairs down to them while looking around. There were only a few other people sitting.

"Hi ladies."

They were each wearing their significant other's jersey, making me just a little bit jealous. Not of who they were with, but that they were with someone. The life of a personal assistant was a lonely one. I lived the life of my client, rarely my own. I didn't have a lot of friends. I had contacts. I didn't have time for myself. I had to be available at any time for their needs.

I hadn't minded all that much, until recently. I was getting sick of seeing my high school and college friends grow up, move away, get married, have kids, all while I was living alone.

I loved my job. I did. But I wanted more.

Maybe these women could be the solution. Maybe they could be my friends.

Chloe started to stand. "Have you eaten yet? We were just about to head up to the banquet level."

"What's up there?" They were picking up their purses, so I kept mine on my shoulder and waited for them.

"They have food and drinks for VIPs." Chloe headed up the stairs and I followed behind with Emma and Sophia.

"And we're VIPs?"

Emma laughed. "Friends, family, agents, invited guests, reporters. They're all included."

I paused on a step. "I'm not really any of those."

"Invited guest. Plus, you're our friend." Sophia turned and winked at me.

I'd never admit how much that meant to me. They included me. They considered me a friend.

"Can we see the ice from up there?"

Emma nodded. "You can see everything."

Sophia turned to me before pressing the elevator button. "Why?"

"I wanted to watch Noah warm up."

The three of them looked at each other, smiling. Chloe was grinning like a fiend. "Why is that, Colby?"

I shrugged. "He was nervous before. I just want to make sure he gets it out of his head."

They slowly nodded, almost in sync.

"Is that all?" Sophia asked.

"Yeah?" What were they trying to hint at? Of course, I wanted to see him warm up. Not that I could do anything at this point, but I wanted him to know I was there.

"We'll see," Chloe whispered to the others, and I pretended not to hear.

7

NOAH

This was the most surreal night of my life. The game had been amazing. I played over fifteen minutes and made some really good blocks. I'd even managed to take possession of the puck and pass it down to Erik. He turned and shot a goal in one motion.

I had an assist in my first game! That was better than I could have dreamed.

I felt I'd done well when the guys started patting me on the back, but when Coach nodded at me as I passed him in the tunnel, I knew. He had the slightest grin and I could feel it in my bones. He was happy with me.

I couldn't wait to talk to my parents. And Colby. I'd seen her in the audience with the Pride. It felt amazing knowing she was there.

"Noah!"

"Malkin."

"Noah, can we get a comment?"

I turned to the voices and backed up a little. The hall leading to the locker room was packed. I couldn't tell who was with the team, who was a reporter, and who was just a fan. It was too much. People were shouting my name, but I couldn't find them in the crowd.

There was nowhere to run. I wanted to get back to the locker room. That would be safe right?

A horde of girls, probably younger than me, broke through the packed crowd and rushed in my direction.

"There he is!"

"Noah!"

One of the girls was crying. Was she hurt? Had she been trampled? "Marry me?"

Oh no.

The minute those words left her mouth my body went into panic mode. Fight or flight.

I couldn't fight these girls, though. I'd have to run.

I moved forward but a hand reached out and grabbed my arm. I looked at it, then connected it to its body. I recognized that shirt. I looked up and felt like I could finally breathe. Colby was here.

"Come on. There are a few people who want to talk to you before you go in."

I nodded. I'd figured that part out, I just couldn't find them.

She pulled me through the hall, away from the crazed pack, until it thinned out a bit. There were five or so men and women with microphones or recorders pointed at me. Colby positioned me in the center then stepped to the side. I reached out for her, but she was too far away. I wanted her close. I felt lost without her.

"Noah, what did you think of your first NHL game?"

I didn't know who asked so I scanned the group and spoke. "It was incredible. Such a rush. The team is amazing and has really been great to work with."

"Noah, you made some impressive saves. Who do you credit for those?"

I almost laughed at the question. Um. Every coach I've had since I could skate. "I've had amazing coaches through the years and working with Coach Romney and Coach Rust has helped me so much."

"Noah, do you think you'll be here next season?"

My heart seized in my chest. "I want nothing more than to be with the Fury next season, but we'll have to wait and see what happens."

I looked around as more questions were shouted at me.

Colby stepped forward. "Okay, Noah has time for one more."

A blonde woman in the front waved her hand. "Noah are you single?"

Colby shook her head and the rest of the group gave the reporter bad looks. I guess they were mad at her wasting the last question on something so dumb. "I..."

"Don't have to answer that. Come on, Noah." I was relieved Colby had stepped in. I was single, but I didn't want everyone to know. It wasn't their business. I couldn't believe anyone would care either.

"Thanks, Colby."

She smiled briefly before pointing me in the direction of the locker room. "Just doing my job."

I shook my head as I walked away. That wasn't a part of her job. Guiding me through the crowd, helping me with reporters? That wasn't what a personal assistant did. That was more of a manager or PR rep. She had gone above and beyond today, and I wanted her to know I appreciated it. Should I get her a present? A bonus?

No. That was too much like I was her boss. I didn't want

her to just think of me that way. I wanted to at least be friends.

I chatted with the guys and thanked each of them who congratulated me before showering and changing back into my suit. Colby was waiting in the hall with Chloe and Reese when I walked out.

"Nice job, Noah. You did really well." Chloe reached out and patted my back.

"Thanks Chloe." Her opinion mattered as much as the guys and coaches. She knew hockey, and from what I'd heard she wouldn't give a compliment unless she meant it.

"Do you guys want to go out with us for dinner?" Reese asked without looking at Chloe, but she was smiling. They must have planned this. I glanced at Colby, but she was indifferent. Was it up to me? Would she feel obligated? Did she want to go?

"Sure, if you're up for it?" I directed my question at her and she nodded. I waited for her to say anything, but that was all the reaction I was going to get.

Reese nodded. "Cool. I want to go get changed into normal clothes. We'll meet you at Chomp in thirty minutes?"

I agreed even though I had no idea what Chomp was.

"See you guys."

We went different directions in the parking garage and Colby got into the passenger seat without a word.

I started the car and turned to her. "Are you okay?"

She smiled and nodded. "Yeah, sorry. Tonight, was a bit much."

I ran a hand through my damp hair. "I know. It was crazy. Thanks so much for being there after the game. I had no idea what I was doing."

She laughed, and her smile finally reached her eyes. "I

noticed. I thought those girls were going to grab you and take you back to their lair."

"That was terrifying." I pulled out of the garage and headed toward home. "I wasn't prepared for that. I didn't think anyone would really notice me or care enough to interview me."

"Oh Noah. You have no idea. The fans went crazy for you."

"Really? More than just the pack of she-wolves?" The crowd had been loud tonight, but it was always that way at the Fury arena.

"Yeah, the fans took notice and I know the media did. It helps that you look like that."

What was that supposed to mean? "Like what?" Should I be offended?

She blushed. Her neck and cheeks reddened, and I realized what she was saying. She thought I was cute. I couldn't help it. I smiled.

When she didn't reply I looked over at her. "What do you mean, Colby?"

I tried to stay serious, but I couldn't keep the teasing out of my voice.

She waved me off and looked out the window.

"Oh no. You don't say something like that then ignore me. Do you mean I'm so hideous that I stand out? People were making fun of me? I knew I should have grown a beard to hide this ugly mug."

She giggled. "You know that's not the reason."

"Good. Cause I can't grow a beard. I can't even manage a decent mustache."

Her laugh deepened. "Please, don't try. That would be so weird."

"Oh, now I'm weird looking? Harsh."

"You know you're not weird looking."

"No. I don't. My self-consciousness is growing with each laugh, Colby."

She put her hand on my arm and squeezed. "You're gorgeous, Noah."

"Gorgeous? That's what you tell a girl! Do I look like a girl?"

"Well with those lashes…"

I narrowed my eyes at her.

"I'm serious! Your eyes are amazing. So crystal blue. And your dimple. Wow."

She pretended to fan herself and I no longer knew if she was kidding.

"You have the whole perfect all-American boy look nailed."

"I'm Canadian."

She rolled her eyes. "You know what I mean. You're incredibly attractive and everyone noticed. I'm sure there will be posters of you up around the city soon. A face like that sells tickets."

I cringed. I was kidding earlier about being self-conscious. I knew from past experience that girls thought I was cute. But she made it seem like it was more. She found me attractive. Not in the generally good-looking way, but she, Colby, was attracted to me.

The thought made me smile.

"Oh boy. I've inflated the ego, haven't I?"

I pulled into the parking garage below my building and parked. "Nah. I'm just a humble boy next door."

She smirked. "Every girl's fantasy."

Was it? Was I her fantasy?

I wanted to tease her about it, but I didn't want to push her. I liked what was happening. The teasing. The laughing.

54

I didn't want her to shut down like she'd been when we got in the car.

"Do you mind coming inside or do you want to wait here?" I pointed over my shoulder then dropped my hand.

"I'll come in." She got out after I turned off the car.

On the way up in the elevator I realized I was getting used to her. It had only been a few days, less than a week, since I met her and already she had wiggled her way into my life.

I liked talking to her. Being around her. She was smart and witty. She knew how to navigate this world and never made me feel dumb for messing up. I just wish I knew where the line was. How much of what she did was because it was her job, and how much was because she wanted to?

I had to believe she liked me a little bit, too. She'd spent the whole day with me. She'd calmed me down, distracted me. That felt like something a friend would do.

But maybe she was just good at her job.

"I'll be fast." I hurried to my room and changed into jeans and a t-shirt. I debated leaving my suit laying out on my bed, but I knew Colby would yell at me if she saw. She was strict about cleanliness and organization. It was good for me, though. She kept me in line.

"All set." I slipped my wallet into my back pocket and walked to the door. I stopped when I heard my voice. "What are you watching?"

I looked at the TV and froze. I was on the screen. I was on ESPN.

It was after the game when they were interviewing me.

My phone vibrated in my pocket, but I ignored it. I was on TV.

"So, ladies and gentlemen we don't know the relationship status of the newest Fury player, but that won't stop the fans from falling in love."

The female reporter was smiling at the camera. It was the same woman from the arena. Was this a new gossip show? Since when did they care about whether or not players were dating?

"This is weird." I felt like I'd stepped into the Twilight Zone.

Colby laughed. "Get used to it."

"I'm not sure I will. Can you change it?"

She flipped through the rest of the sports channels, and I was on almost all of them. What was happening?

"Is this real?"

"Welcome to the big leagues, Malkin." She stood from the couch and offered me the remote.

"Nah. Turn it off. This is too weird."

She did and tossed the remote on the couch. "Do you still want to go?"

"Yeah, of course."

I followed her out and back to the car. "Do you know where Chomp is?"

"Yeah, head back toward the arena."

I followed her directions until she told me to park. We walked into the small, diner style restaurant and saw Chloe waving to us. I wasn't sure what I was expecting, maybe a fancy cloth napkin kind of place. This was much more low-key. Something I was comfortable with. There weren't too many people in the booths, and they didn't seem to care about me or Reese.

"Hey guys." I scooted into the large, round booth leaving room for Colby to sit next to me.

"Is anyone else coming?" Colby asked looking around at

the empty space. She was right. It looked too big for just the four of us.

"Yeah, my brother and his fiancé, Madeline, are coming."

This was the first time I'd be hanging out with the guys, as just me. Not as a team or big group. Just me. Noah.

I tried not to show my excitement, but this was a big deal for me. This was the first step to being accepted by them. Colby and Chloe were chatting about shopping or clothes or something, so I glanced at Reese. I didn't really know what to say to him. He was still a hero in my mind. Not someone I should be sharing a booth with.

"You did really well tonight. Those were some great blocks. Keep that up and Olli will start asking for you on the first line."

I clenched my jaw to keep my mouth from falling open. They'd noticed me? Did he really think Olli liked me?

I was sounding like a teenage girl talking about her crush. I needed to calm down. I was on their team. I was one of them. I might not believe it yet, but I was good enough to be here.

"Thanks. I'll try."

Reese nodded before looking past me.

"Hey guys." A male voice called out.

I turned to see Erik and a beautiful blonde walking our direction. Colby patted my leg and started moving closer, so I scooted to the middle to make room for the new arrivals.

"Hi, Noah. I'm Madeline." She reached across the table and offered her hand. I shook it and gestured to Colby.

"Madeline, this is Colby."

They exchanged hellos before she and Erik sat down.

"It's nice to finally meet you, Colby. Chloe's been talking nonstop about her new friend," Erik said.

Colby blushed, and I couldn't tell if it was from his words or his proximity. Erik was one of the stars of the team, and from what I've heard, every woman's favorite player.

"It's nice to meet you too."

She didn't sound flustered, like a fan would. I eyed him and scooted closer to Chloe to give Colby more space from Erik.

"Noah, I think I owe you a drink for that goal."

He smiled, and the group laughed.

"Maybe a root beer tonight." Madeline winked. I was glad there wasn't any pressure to drink. I wasn't old enough and I didn't want to remind them of that.

"Sounds good."

Erik nodded and turned to talk to Chloe. Colby and Madeline began talking about their work while I studied the menu. Not that there was much to consider. The place specialized in burgers. I didn't know who to talk to or how to break into a conversation. I was jealous Colby seemed comfortable meeting new people and immediately getting to know them. I wouldn't be surprised if by the end of the night she and Madeline exchanged numbers and had plans for another night.

"Noah, what do you think?"

I looked up from the menu to see everyone staring at me. I had no idea what Colby was asking about.

"Sorry?"

"Erik and Chloe are hosting a dinner this weekend and invited us. Do you think you can make it?"

I pretended to think about it. As if I had so many plans and previous commitments to think about. Colby knew I didn't have anything going on, but maybe she wanted to make sure I was okay with it. That was nice of her.

"Yeah, shouldn't be a problem. Thanks guys."

"Chloe's always planning something, so be prepared for constant events or dinners." Reese sounded bored but laughed when Chloe stuck her elbow in his ribs.

"It's true. I don't think I've been to so many parties in my life, until I moved here." Madeline laughed. "I think she'd break down if she didn't have something to plan."

Chloe rolled her eyes. "It's my job you guys."

Erik shook his head. "For the team. Not for us."

She shrugged. "When have any of you guys not had fun with me?"

Reese slid his arm around her shoulders. "You're right. You do make sure everyone's having a good time."

She nodded then smiled as the waitress came to our table.

"Are you guys ready to order?"

We went around the table ordering our various burgers then she walked away.

"Noah, where are you from?"

Madeline was the one to ask, probably because she was the only one who didn't know. "Vancouver, Canada."

Her eyes lit up and she looked to Erik. "Is that close to where you grew up?"

He laughed and shook his head. "Not even in the same province."

The rest of the table laughed, even Colby.

Madeline just shrugged. "Canada's all the same to me."

"Classic American." Reese joked.

Madeline leaned forward. "What about you, Colby? Where are you from?"

I sat up a bit. I didn't even know the answer. Why hadn't I thought to ask before now? I thought about it for a second and realized I didn't know much of anything about her. I hadn't bothered to ask. Yet, she seemed to know, or learn, everything about me.

"I'm originally from Northern California but came here for school. I fell in love with the mountains and the four seasons and decided to stay." She smiled but I could tell there was something more. Something she wasn't saying. I'd have to ask her about it later, when we were alone.

"Is your family still out there?" Madeline asked and everyone waited

"Yeah."

Madeline nodded. "It must be hard to be away from them. I knew it was for me."

Colby shrugged. "We're not that close."

I'd have to add that to the list of things I needed to ask about.

No one said anything for a beat.

"What brought you here, Madeline?" Colby asked while I absorbed the conversation.

"My dad is the coach."

I froze. What? How did I not know that?

Colby grinned. "Oh really? Rust or Romney?"

"Romney."

I needed to get out of here. I suddenly felt like a spotlight was on me. Not the stage kind. The kind interrogators used to force people to confess. How were the other guys okay hanging out with her? Wasn't everything they said or did reported back?

I was sweating.

Madeline and Colby continued to talk about mundane things while I silently freaked out. This was too much. I wasn't ready to be around these people. I wasn't worthy. I hadn't paid my dues.

They were probably used to being around Coach. They didn't have anything to fear. I was the only one on thin ice.

Colby didn't seem to notice my inner battle and continued asking questions. "How long have you been on the team Erik?"

"Four years."

"And you like it here?"

"I love it." He put his arm around his fiancé and they smiled. "I hope to stay here for my career."

"Is that normal for hockey players?"

He shrugged. "It can happen. It's definitely more common than in basketball."

Colby nodded. "That's what I'm used to."

Madeline perked up. "Did you date a player?"

What? Why would that be her first conclusion?

Colby laughed. "Oh no. I've worked for a few."

Madeline still looked confused.

"I'm a personal assistant."

"Oh." With the way her eyebrows shot up I figured she didn't know that before. Why wouldn't Chloe have told her? She eyed me before looking back to Colby.

"I bet you have some interesting stories to tell."

Colby laughed again. "Not as many as you'd think. My clients have been pretty easy so far."

"How about now?" Reese asked with a smirk. I narrowed my eyes at him, but no one seemed to notice.

"Noah's great. It's a new world for me though. I didn't know much about hockey before meeting him."

Madeline gaped. "Wait. You're his personal assistant?"

Colby nodded while I eyed the blonde. Why was that surprising?

"Sorry, you guys just look so comfortable with each other. I assumed..." She shook her head and looked around the table, but no one else said anything. "Sorry. I thought you were a personal assistant for another athlete and that's how you two met."

"Oh no. We're not together." Colby waved her hands while I decided if I should be offended by how quickly she dismissed the possibility.

"Huh." Madeline smiled, looking confused.

Huh? What was that supposed to mean? I wanted to demand answers, but our waitress came with our food and the topic died.

I ate in silence wondering what she meant by that. We looked comfortable together? Did we? I mean, we'd spent a lot of time together in the past few days. But it was all business. Was it weird for me to be hanging out with my assistant? I didn't know. I'd never had one and didn't know anyone who did.

Maybe there was a line I was supposed to draw. Keep some distance between us. But I didn't want that. I liked how things were. In fact, I wouldn't mind if we got closer.

Colby didn't seem to mind the question though. She ate and laughed and talked with everyone like nothing was wrong.

So, it was me. I was the one left out, confused, and questioning everything.

I hated feeling this way. Like I was out of control. Out of the loop.

"Hey! It's Noah!" Chloe pointed to a TV screen hanging over a booth a few feet away. My face was on the screen with a quote I couldn't read.

Erik nudged my shoulder and smiled while Reese held up a hand for a high five. "I bet that doesn't happen every day."

I returned the high five and shook my head. "This is pretty surreal."

Erik nodded. "It took a while to get used to it, but pretty soon your face will be everywhere, and you'll stop noticing."

"I don't think I will."

Colby grabbed my arm. "It will be okay. I know this seems crazy now, but this attention comes with being in the NHL."

I nodded. I couldn't do much else. It was like I was in a different world. Or living someone else's life. Someday this might all click, but not at this moment.

I looked up to see Madeline staring at Colby's hand on me. When she saw me watching her she smiled and winked.

That woman. She was going to drive me crazy. It wasn't like I could ask to talk to her alone. Not unless I wanted to face Erik's wrath, but what was with all the looks and little comments?

I tried to ignore it and finish my burger, but I lost my appetite. No one seemed to notice. They finished and kept talking and laughing until finally, Reese stood.

"I don't know about you guys, but I'm exhausted."

Everyone followed, and the guys tossed cash on the table. I reached for my wallet and added a twenty to the table.

Colby hugged the girls and said goodbye before following me to the car. "That was a fun night, thanks for inviting me."

"Yeah." I opened her door and waited for her to get in before walking around to the driver's side. At least she had a good time. For some reason, that mattered to me.

8

COLBY

Noah seemed different, off, all night but I didn't want to push him. There was a lot for him to take in. His first NHL game, the press afterward, going to dinner with his teammates, and seeing his face on TV. That was more than any person should have to handle in one week, let alone one day.

I let him think on the drive home. Letting him process, but once we parked back at his place he didn't move to turn off the car or get out. I waited. I didn't want to push him. He didn't ask me to leave either, so I sat in silence.

"Tell me about your family."

The question caught me off guard. I looked at him, but he was staring straight ahead. At the cement wall.

"My parents are still together. They live in a suburb of San Francisco, where I grew up."

"Any siblings?"

"An older sister. Amy. She's married and has two kids. She lives about thirty minutes from my parents."

"Are they sad you don't live there too?"

I waited for him to look at me, but he was frozen. "Probably not. I doubt they care." I cleared my throat. "I haven't really been home since I left for college."

He raised a brow and I continued. "We were never very close. Business and obligations always came first. I was mostly raised by nannies. My parents aren't the sentimental type. They're just happy I have a career."

"So, you don't want to go back?"

"Not necessarily. I want to be where my work takes me. I love Salt Lake. Even though the snow can suck sometimes, I love being here."

"Okay." With that he took out the keys and opened his door. Just like that I guess the conversation was over. I wanted to ask him about his family, but now wasn't the time.

At the back of the car I said goodbye. I watched him walk away to the elevator. His shoulders were slumped, his head was down. This wasn't the Noah I knew. His charisma was gone. I could only hope he was just overwhelmed from the day. He'd rest and be back to normal.

I walked to my car and headed home. I was walking through my front door when my phone rang.

It was Bryce.

Why would he be calling me? At close to midnight?

Oh no. Something happened to Noah. He was jumped. His house was broken into. He fell and broke his leg.

Hundreds of horrible situations ran through my mind before I could tell myself to answer the call.

"Hello?"

"Colby. I've got news."

"What is it?" I tried to keep the panic out of my voice, but I knew he could hear it.

"You need to pack your bags."

"What?" This was so much worse than I could have imagined. I was being fired. That was why Noah had been so quiet around me. He was firing me. He couldn't even do it himself. He made his agent call me? Anger flooded through me.

What had I done? Had I said something at dinner?

Was that why he was asking about my family? Probably making sure I had somewhere to go when I was broke and homeless. Goodbye money. Goodbye dreams of being debt free. Goodbye business plan.

"You're moving."

What? "Where?"

"In with Noah."

My head was spinning. What was he talking about? "Did something happen? Is he safe?"

Why would they want me to move in? If there was a security threat, they needed to hire a bodyguard. Not me. I'd break my hand trying to punch someone.

"Noah's fine. For now."

There really was a threat! I wasn't prepared for this! I could get dry cleaning and organize his schedule. I couldn't protect the guy!

"What's going on, Bryce?"

"There's been a surge of attention on Noah that we didn't anticipate."

"I saw him on the news tonight."

"Yes, he's all over the local and national news. His face is all over the internet. There are already fan groups forming. People saying they're going to stalk him. Marry him."

I stopped in the hallway. "You're telling me he has fans?"

"Yes."

"And this is cause for concern?"

Bryce sighed. "In this case, yes. Look, Colby. You and I are both more experienced with this sort of thing. We know what to expect, we know how things work. Noah doesn't.

66

He's like an innocent child. We need to protect him. Mostly, from himself. I don't want this fame going to his head."

I didn't want that either. Money and fame that came too fast and too soon has led good people down very bad paths. I didn't want to see Noah get lost in that. He was too good.

"What would moving in with him do? I can make sure he doesn't watch TV but it's not like I can take away his phone."

"You're not going there for that."

"Then what?" He was speaking in code and it was getting on my last nerve.

"You're going to be his girlfriend."

I fell against the doorframe leading to my room. "What?"

"You're going to pretend to be his girlfriend."

"Why?"

"If you two are photographed together and he talks about you in interviews, I think some of the unwanted attention will die down. Plus, you'll be able to keep an even closer eye on him. Make sure he's not hanging around the wrong people or making any stupid decisions."

"I can't date my clients, Bryce. How am I supposed to build a reputable career if I date one of athletes? No one will take me seriously." I had a hard enough time as a woman in this field trying to work her way up. I couldn't risk ruining my reputation or having people think I was unprofessional.

"No one will know you work for him. You'll keep your other clients and I'll spread a story that you guys met at an event."

"The team already knows who I am. I can't make sure none of them say anything."

"Let me deal with that. You just need to keep up the façade until things calm down."

I rubbed my forehead trying to get the information to process. "Does he know?"

"Yes."

"He agreed?" He was probably just listening to whatever Bryce said.

"Of course. I wouldn't be calling you if he didn't." Yes, he would. If he thought it was the best decision, he'd go through with it no matter what either of us said.

"For how long?"

"Who knows? Until the attention around him dies down."

"Then we'll have a pretend breakup?"

"Sure, I doubt people will care at that point. You can move back to your place and go back to normal."

"Why am I having to move in with him?"

"Because there are already cameras outside his building. If we want you two to be taken seriously you have to live with each other."

"There are plenty of serious couples who don't live with each other."

"That's true. But you are not one of them."

"Bryce, I'm not moving in with him."

"It's not negotiable, Colby."

I shook my head. I wasn't going to let him dictate my life. I might be under contract with him, but this was not included.

"No."

"What?"

"I'll be over there as much as I can. I'll keep an eye on him. Make sure he doesn't get in over his head, but living with him is out of the question."

"We'll double the pay for the time you live with him."

What? That was unbelievable. Noah couldn't afford that.

But Bryce could. It must mean a lot if he was willing to pay me to do this.

I could use the money. My student loans would disappear in a few months if I went through with this. No more worrying about being able to pay rent. No more taking on too much work just to make ends meet. I could actually get ahead. Build my business.

"Bryce, I don't feel comfortable moving in."

There was a long pause. I checked my screen to make sure the call was still connected.

"Fine."

"Fine?" Did that mean I didn't have to or that I was fired?

"You don't have to move in." I sighed and felt like I could take a breath for the first time during this phone call. "But I want you around. As much as possible, Colby. I mean it. If he's going to the store, you're with him. If he's making an appearance, you're on his elbow. Do you understand?"

"Yes, of course."

He sighed. "I'll still double your pay for the next two months."

I couldn't believe it. I thought I was going to get fired for standing up to him and now I was getting the raise?

"Thank you so much, sir."

"There's a lot riding on him right now, Colby. Don't let him make a single mistake. There are too many eyes on him."

"I understand."

"And remember this is a professional relationship. Do what you have to for the cameras, but your job is managing him and his image. Don't forget that."

He didn't need to say the words for me to understand his meaning. Nothing could happen between us. Not for real.

"Okay. Have a good night, Colby."

I hung up and dropped my head against the wall. Again. And again.

What had I gotten myself into?

I sent Noah a text to let him know the plans had changed.

His response came in a minute later. He wanted to talk. Lovely.

I turned around and headed back out the door.

Once I got back to his building I parked and looked around, but I didn't see anyone in the garage. I took my bag and hurried to the elevator.

Worrying about paparazzi was new for me. I'd have to pay more attention to what I was wearing and if I'd washed my hair now. This was probably something Chloe and Madeline were used to. I'd have to talk to them later about it. See if they had any tips or tricks.

I couldn't believe this was happening.

A fake relationship?

It was weirder that I'd agreed to it. It was the best thing for Noah. And he was my client, so I had to keep his best interest in mind. Even if that meant putting my life on pause for the money and for however long his moment lasted.

Remember the money, Colby.

What if the Fury signed him? What if he was here for good, and the people loved him? What would that mean for us? Would we have to stay together? No. That was ludicrous.

He'd break up with me at some point, so he could date for real. Probably models.

Great. Making myself upset over unknown futures was not something I needed right now.

I got off the elevator and walked down to Noah's. He was waiting for me with the door cracked open.

"Hey girlfriend."

His smile was back. He seemed like he was happy. Hopefully whatever funk he was in was over.

"Hi boyfriend." I laughed at his goofy smile. "This is so weird."

"What? You don't want to date me?" He pretended to be offended but ended up smiling. "You're right, this is weird." He stepped forward wrapping me in an awkward hug. As weird and forced as it felt, I kind of didn't mind. I mean, getting to be in his arms wasn't such a bad thing. I inhaled and mentally slapped myself. No enjoying myself. No melting into him. This was business.

"Come on in."

I followed silently. Sure I'd been in his apartment, but I suddenly felt out of place. Like there was a new meaning to being here. Which there wasn't. Everything was the same. Kind of.

"Hungry?" Noah called as he walked into the kitchen.

We'd just eaten, but Noah always seemed to be hungry. Probably all the exercising he did. I bet a game made it even worse.

"Maybe."

I looked in, between his arm and the door, but there was very little food. We hadn't gone back to the store together, but I'd been back to keep up the stock of his favorites.

"Do you want me to go grab something?"

He turned his head and looked at me over his shoulder. He froze as his eyes dropped to my lips for a moment before meeting my eyes.

"No, it's okay. I was just hoping ice cream, or something had appeared."

"You told me no sugar."

He shut the doors and faced me with his arms crossed. "I know. I just crave it sometimes."

"But you don't want to eat it."

He shook his head. "No, I shouldn't."

"You're so strong. I'd cave after one day of no sugar."

He shrugged. "I know I feel better and perform better when I'm eating clean."

"So, if I told you I have a candy bar in my purse, you wouldn't want to share?"

His eyes narrowed. "You're lying."

I slowly shook my head and took steps backward to the living room. He grinned and shoved past me.

"You won't look in a woman's purse." I yelled but he was already gone. I laughed and hurried, but when I caught up he was holding the chocolate above his head like it was a trophy. He was trying to look intimidating, probably to keep me from going after it, but I couldn't help but laugh. "Give it back, Noah. You don't want to do this."

His lips twitched. He was trying not to smile. "I think I do."

I took one step forward, keeping my hands out like I was approaching a dangerous animal. "Noah. You just said you feel better when you don't."

"That was before you told me you brought chocolate into the house."

"You can't go from no sugar to a full candy bar. You'll make yourself sick."

"No, I won't."

Now he was sounding like a defiant child. "Noah. Set the bar on the ground."

He shook his head.

"Noah, at least share it with me."

He shook his head as he raised his other hand up and ripped the wrapper open.

"Noah!"

Slowly, he lowered one hand to his mouth.

"Don't."

He licked it and when his eyes closed I ran at him, tackling him onto the sofa.

He grunted, and the chocolate went flying to the other side of the room. "Hey! You can't do that."

"I just did. And you'll thank me later."

He shifted, and I realized I was straddling his waist. His hands shot up, immediately finding my tickle spot on my ribs. I flailed, trying to get away, but he tightened his hold and lifted me off him before tossing me to the side of the sofa. He scrambled to get up, but I threw myself over his legs, stopping him.

"No!"

He pulled himself to end of the sofa with his arms, dragging me along. "Yes. I need it."

"No, you don't." I wrapped both arms around his legs, but he didn't seem to notice. We were sliding again until his torso was hanging off. I knew he had to be close, so I released one arm and reached up to grab his side.

He shrieked, like a little girl, and fell off the couch.

I was laughing too hard to follow him. I'd never heard such a noise from a grown man. His head popped up next to mine. "What's so funny?"

His mouth was full of chocolate and I slapped his arm. All of that fighting and I still lost.

"You screamed like a girl!"

"No, I didn't."

He shoved the candy in my open mouth and I quickly took a bite.

"Ha!" I laughed with a full mouth, struggling to breathe. I could feel him next to me and I realized what I'd just done. That was the opposite of professional.

I bit back my smile. But I'd like it.

Noah sat on the ground, next to me, and finished the bar. "You're a horrible influence on me."

"You just have no self-control."

"Nah, it's all you. I'm going to call Bryce and tell him how horrible you are."

I smacked his shoulder. "Then he'll have to get you a new girlfriend. One who never, ever has sweets."

He shuddered. "No way. I'm keeping you."

"Good to know you only like me for one reason."

"Your pretty smile?"

My breath caught. Did he mean that? I forced myself to ignore it. "No."

"Your long hair?"

He was so close. Looking into my eyes in a way I hadn't experienced before. "Nope."

"Your dashing personality."

I laughed. "Of course not."

"You're wrong. You're good for more than just candy."

I looked over at him, upside down. "Yeah?"

"Yeah. You can make me laugh."

I smiled. "That's not such a bad thing."

He shook his head and slowly smiled. "No, it's really not."

I looked around the room, remembering why I was here. "About the arrangement."

He nodded. "You don't want to live with me?" He pouted and I almost smacked him.

"I don't think that's a good idea."

He wagged his eyebrows. "Can't resist me."

Warmth flooded over me and I prayed he didn't notice my blush. "I just don't think it's professional."

He fell back against the sofa. "Okay, I understand, but you're still going to be my girlfriend?"

He sounded a little too happy about it.

"Yes."

"Cool." His grin sent a shiver down my spine. This was such a terrible idea.

"We need rules."

"Rules?"

I nodded. "Ground rules. What is allowed and what isn't."

"So what are they?"

"No kissing."

He stared at me for a moment before laughing. "I'm not supposed to kiss my girlfriend? That doesn't make any sense."

Fine. He was right. It just wasn't going to make things any easier on me. "Okay, but only when we know there are cameras around."

He agreed.

"Hand holding is fine. If reporters ask for information we just tell them no comment. We'll have to ask the rest of the team to do the same."

"Okay. I want you to come to my practices and games."

I already knew it meant a lot for me to be there. I think he needed to know there was at least one person rooting for him. "Deal. And if anything else comes up, we'll figure it out."

"You don't need to make it sound so dreadful." He shot me a playful look. "We can actually have fun together."

I smiled. I hadn't meant to make it sound like a terrible chore. "Okay."

His grin grew. "Sounds good, girlfriend."

9

NOAH

Bryce was right about the sudden attention he predicted I'd be getting. Paparazzi were stationed outside my building in the morning. I had on sunglasses and a hat, hoping to go unnoticed, but once they saw my car the cameras started flashing.

I didn't get it. I was a rookie.

I bet they'd disappear within the week. It wasn't like I was doing anything interesting. They could take all the pictures they wanted of me coming and going to practice. They'd probably die of boredom. If they wanted scandal, they chose the wrong player.

When I got to the arena there were a few people with cameras waiting, but I'd noticed that happened a few times. This was the place to capture shots of all the players. In their cars.

Now I understood why there were private practices. If they got inside it would never end. We needed space. Time to focus. Erik told me Chloe kept a sharp eye out for anyone coming into the arena who didn't belong. She didn't want distractions around. Whether it was a reporter or a one-night stand. She wanted us to be able to tune it all out and be present for practice.

I appreciated it. Especially, now that there was some attention on me. Erik and Reese greeted me in the locker room and it was cool to feel welcomed. I felt a little more official. Like I was really becoming one of them. Baby steps.

Colby was sitting with Chloe, working on her laptop in the audience. She waved when she caught me looking, then went back to work. I appreciated her coming for me. Ever since the first day when I asked her to come, she hadn't missed.

Practice was still rough. I was sore every day, even after repeated ice baths. I was getting used to it though. It was worth it. Seeing it pay off during the game made me realize how important it was to lay it all out every day. If we pushed ourselves hard now, we'd be ready come game time.

When the final whistle blew I joined Brassard and Hartman in the gym to stretch and roll our sore muscles.

"Have you been getting hounded?"

I looked up to see Brassard looking at me.

"You mean the paps?"

He nodded and cringed while rolling out his calf.

"They were at my building this morning, but it wasn't bad."

"It's going to get worse." Hartman was smirking when I met his eyes.

"Why?"

"A friend of mine from Sports Today magazine said they're doing a full spread on you and have named you this season's number one rookie to keep an eye on."

I threw my head back. "Great."

"Hey, this is good for you. If you bring in good press and help with sales, the team will notice. You want a contract, don't you?" Brassard was right. I shouldn't complain about this.

"But won't they need a photo shoot for that?"

Hartman shrugged. "They must have enough pictures already."

Wonderful. Probably embarrassing shots from old teams.

"Don't sweat it. They'll move on eventually. In the meantime, use it. Get your name out there. Prove to the management that you're someone they need on the team."

No wonder he was the captain. He knew how to work this. I could use it to my advantage, and I knew Colby would know exactly how to do that.

I hurried through the motions of showering and getting dressed. Colby normally left after practice, so I wanted to get home to talk to her. Knowing she would be home, at my home, waiting for me was pretty great. I'd have to send Bryce a gift basket or something for coming up with this arrangement.

When I opened the door, I heard noise coming from the kitchen. I dropped my bag and went toward the sound. Colby was bent over in front of the fridge.

"What are you looking for?"

She jumped and turned. "You scared me."

Her expression made me laugh. "Sorry, I thought you heard me."

She glared at me before turning back to the fridge. "I got everything to make a salad, but I can't find the feta I bought."

"I moved it to the drawer."

She pulled it out and set everything on the counter. "Hungry?"

I sat down on one of the bar stools and nodded. "Always."

"I'll get to work then."

"You don't have to cook for me."

She stopped and smiled. "I know. Thanks. I'm going to this time because I'm hungry too."

"Fair enough."

I watched her move around the kitchen like she's lived here forever. I loved the way her hair flowed out behind her. It always looked so soft. Silky. I wanted to run my hands through it.

"Noah?"

I blinked and looked up at her. "What?"

"I said do you want chicken or steak?"

"Steak."

I wanted to shake myself. I needed to pull it together. I couldn't zone out staring at her. She'd notice and get creeped out.

I cleared my throat. "Hey, Hartman said something today and I think it's a good idea."

She pulled a cutting board from a lower cabinet and set it on the counter. "What's the idea?"

"He said I should take advantage of all the attention on me right now. He said I should use it to bring in money for the team. To show them I can be beneficial."

She nodded as she chopped a head of Romaine lettuce. "That's a good idea."

"Do you know how I can do that?"

She continued working in silence for a minute. "We should have you make some appearances."

"Like talk shows?"

She held up a tomato and I nodded. "Maybe. I think people need to see you. Hear from you. They need to know

79

who Noah Malkin is. What he's about. What he likes. We need to make you real to them."

That made sense to me. It was hard to cheer for someone you didn't know.

"How do we do that?"

"I'll get you some interviews. But we can start small. You need to be seen."

She added all of the chopped vegetables to a bowl and flipped the steaks she had on a cast iron pan.

"I'll talk to Chloe. She'll know the best places to go and she might even know of some events for you to attend. Rubbing elbows with the right people can go a long way."

"Thanks, Colby."

She glanced up and gave me a brief smile. "Of course."

"Will you be there with me?"

She paused. "If you want me to."

"Well, you are my girlfriend, so it might be weird if you weren't."

She laughed then shook her head. "I feel like Bryce made a mistake there. He probably only suggested me since I was already available, but I don't think It will be believable."

"What won't?"

"Me with you."

I was confused. She was beautiful, and I'd been told I have a baby face. She probably didn't think people would believe she would date someone like me.

She looked at me like it was obvious. When I didn't say anything, she sighed. "Fine, you're going to make me say it out loud." She stuck a large wooden fork and spoon in the bowl and began tossing it, will a bit too much vigor. "People aren't going to believe you are dating a girl like me."

80

So, it was just like I thought. I wasn't good enough for her. I was such an idiot.

"I mean, I'm an average girl. There's nothing special about me. They'll probably do some digging and figure out I'm a PA and assume I just work for you."

"Wait, what?"

She tilted her head and gave me a condescending look. "Noah, people aren't going to believe we're a couple."

I approached her until her eyes widened, my chest inches from hers. "I can do it if you can. I can stare at you like no one else matters, stay by your side like I can't get enough of you." She was frozen. Speechless for the first time since we'd met. "Will that work?"

She nodded slowly. "Yeah."

"Unless it will be too hard for you to pretend you're attracted to me." I paused waiting for her reaction.

She sputtered. "You?" A giggle escaped. " You look like a Greek god and the American dream had a baby together."

I laughed. "That doesn't even make sense."

She finally smiled. "Yes, it does. You've got the body of a Greek god, but the face of the boy you can bring home to meet your parents."

I narrowed my eyes. "I feel like I should be offended."

Her wonderful blush returned, and I couldn't help but smile. I'd done that. "Thanks, Noah."

"It helps that you know how to cook, too."

She rolled her eyes and turned around to take the steaks off the stove. I couldn't take my eyes off her. We'd both admitted we found the other attractive. That was a good sign. I just had to get her to see me as more than just a client. More than even a friend.

Maybe this pretending wouldn't be so bad. I'd get to hold her hand. Kiss her. I mean, that's what couples did.

People would think it was weird if we didn't. I didn't want to blow our cover. I smiled even though I knew she would challenge me on that.

But we couldn't let the press know we're faking it. That would be horrible. Imagine the press I'd get if they found out I was faking a relationship.

Suddenly, things were looking a whole lot better.

She slid a plate in front of me before walking around the counter to sit next to me.

"After this I think we should probably go out somewhere."

She swallowed her bite before responding. "Where?"

I shrugged. I hadn't thought that far ahead. "Somewhere public."

"So, they can get some pictures?"

"Yeah." See she thought it was a good idea too. Probably.

"Sure, we should probably give them something, so they leave you alone sooner."

I had wanted that up until about four minutes ago. Now I wanted them around. Then I would have an excuse for being close to her. I felt like an evil genius. My plan was coming together. Cue evil laughter.

10

COLBY

After we ate and cleaned up the kitchen, we headed out. There was a park across the street we could go explore, but I think it was also to make sure the paps saw us.

"I'm going to get a coat."

I waited for him by the door looking down at my boots and jeans. I'd put on my maroon pea coat, so hopefully it photographed well. I wished I could put on a cute outfit, but it was too cold. I grabbed a grey beanie and pulled that on.

"Ready?"

Noah looked great in his grey coat and black jeans. His body was really so close to perfection it was ridiculous. And unfair. Okay he worked hard for it, but I still envied him.

"Yeah let's go."

"Remember the rules."

He rolled his eyes. "How about we just wing it."

He winked and turned. I followed him down the hall, and I may have glanced at his butt. Maybe. I would never admit it to anyone, but I couldn't help it. He was more than cute like I'd told him.

"Do you think they're out there?" I looked through the glass to the street but didn't see anyone.

"Hopefully." He slipped his hand into mine and pulled me to the doors. I looked down at our conjoined hands, not quite sure how I felt about it.

His calloused fingers felt foreign, but familiar at the same time. Like something I wanted to know. It was almost too much to take in. I couldn't pull away though. Especially if there were cameras around. I didn't want them to think we weren't anything but the perfect couple.

We stepped out and the cold air slapped me in the face. Yes, walking in the park was a wonderful idea.

It hadn't snowed recently, but there was just enough snow and ice on the sidewalk to make walking an extreme sport.

"I've got you." I looked up to see him smiling down at me with a look I hadn't seen before. It was more than kind. More than friendship.

I smiled and looked away.

"Noah."

"Mr. Malkin."

"Who's with you?"

There they were. Within a few steps we were surrounded by at least eight cameras and people shouting at him.

"Hi. This is my girlfriend."

I cringed. What happened to the no comment policy? I guess we were making the declaration.

"What's her name?"

I squeezed his hand. This was it. Within hours they'd know everything about me. I'd gone through my electronic footprint and cleaned up anything I didn't want to get out and made sure there was no mention of me working with

84

Noah. Just previous clients. I hoped they wouldn't make the connection.

"This is Colby. We're actually headed for a walk." He started walking, keeping me close to his side. The group spread and followed us across the street. I knew we should be talking. It would seem weird if we walked in silence, but I didn't know what to say. The feeling of being watched was something new for me.

"Have you talked to Madeline since dinner?" It was a random question for him to ask, but I appreciated the distraction. A normal conversation helped make this whole situation feel a lot less weird.

"Yeah, she called me to see if I wanted to have dinner with her and some of the other women this weekend while you guys are traveling."

"Oh nice. That will be fun."

It was really nice of her to reach out. She could have just had Chloe ask, so it meant a lot to me that she would make the effort.

"Yeah, where are you guys going again?"

I knew it was Colorado, but I couldn't think of anything else to ask.

"Denver. We'll only be there for one night."

I smiled and looked up at him. I heard clicking behind me, but I pushed it out of my head. "So, I only have to miss you for a little while."

He looked surprised but quickly recovered. "Yeah baby."

He leaned down and kissed my forehead and I pretty much died right there. In front of him and our entourage.

Who knew a kiss over a beanie could be so amazing? I was embarrassed by how much I enjoyed it. I hadn't been kissed in over a year.

That realization made me pause. Had it really been that

long? Life had picked up. I'd been busy, but surely it hadn't been a year.

I thought back. It was senior year. Before the holiday break. Yeah. Over a year.

"You okay?"

I nodded and kept walking. Words had left my brain. I knew how to speak, right? Had his kiss caused brain damage?

Focus Colby!

"Um... Do you want to get a coffee or hot chocolate?"

He grinned. "Of course."

His smile reassured me. This was Noah. My friend. I blew out a breath and smiled. "They better have sugar free."

He laughed and changed our direction. "I saw a little shop this way."

"Is it this cold in Vancouver?"

"It's close to the coast, so it doesn't get quite as cold, but it snows."

"Do you miss it?"

He shrugged, bringing my hand up with his. "A little bit. I miss my family."

"I'm sorry. When was the last time you got to see them?"

He looked away. "The draft."

That was almost two years ago. "I'm sorry."

He shrugged. "It's the life I choose. I moved around so much as a teen for different teams that I haven't really lived at home since I was about fourteen."

"Wow. I knew you were in the major juniors, but I didn't make the connection of what that would mean for you."

"I was home for the summers, but even then, I was off at camps or training with specialized coaches."

"That must have been hard as a kid."

He nodded. "I grew up fast."

"Yet, you need help grocery shopping?"

He laughed. "I had people around to help with that kind of stuff. I haven't ever lived completely on my own. Back in Boise I lived with three other players. I contributed to the grocery fund and they took care of shopping."

"Oh Noah. That's pathetic. I have so much to teach you."

He turned a corner, then opened the door for me to a small café. Luckily, our shadows didn't follow us in, so we had a short break.

When we got to the counter he turned to me. "What would you like?"

"Oh. I can get it myself."

He shot me a look. "The cameras are on us. I can't have my girlfriend buy her own drink. Plus, I wouldn't have you do that anyway. I asked you out. I pay."

"This is out? Like a date?"

He nodded. "Yeah. It's our first date."

That made me smile. It was a simple date, but it was perfect. Once we got our drinks we went back outside.

"I saw a sign for the aviary, do you want go?"

I froze. He was a few steps ahead when he realized I wasn't next to him. He turned around and gave me a weird look.

"What's wrong?"

I started shaking my head and closed my eyes. I needed to calm down. No freaking out with multiple cameras pointed at me.

"I'd rather not go." I opened my eyes to see his narrow. He took a few steps closer to me.

"Okay, that's fine. We don't have to."

I nodded, not trusting my voice to speak without shaking. He came closer and put his hands on my shoulders. "What's wrong?"

I swallowed and looked up to his eyes. "I don't like birds."

I expected him to laugh or at least smile. He didn't, he pulled me closer and wrapped his arms around me, resting his head on mine. "I finally found a weakness. I was getting worried. I thought maybe you were perfect."

I laughed into his chest. I appreciated him being understanding and not making fun of me. Trying to take my mind off it helped.

"I know it's lame, but I've had a real fear of them for as long as I could remember."

"Then we'll stay far, far away."

He kissed the top of my head and moved to the side, still keeping an arm draped over my shoulder. I missed feeling him around me. That was the closest we've ever been, and I liked it. Probably a little too much.

This was fake. We weren't really together. The clicking of the cameras behind us reminded me of that.

"Let's go take a look at the pond."

"It's frozen."

He rubbed my arm. "All the more reason to check it out. We can come back in the spring to see the difference."

He thought we would still be together in the spring?

Wait. Of course, I was his personal assistant. I would still be around, but that didn't mean we would be an us, a couple.

He placed his arm around my shoulders, pulling me in. We'd only gone a few steps when he paused and looked at me. A smile tugged at his lips a split second before he bent down and kissed me. Again.

I was frozen. His hand left my shoulder and cupped my

cheek. That was enough to break me out of the fog. I lifted my arms and wrapped them around his neck.

The kiss deepened, and my knees turned to mush. This was too much. He was too much.

Kissing a client shouldn't feel like this.

It shouldn't come as naturally as breathing.

He pulled back and smiled. "Sorry. I couldn't resist."

I wanted to tell him to take it easy, but words were hard. My brain was off on cloud nine.

Part of me wanted to distance myself. Protect myself from the impending heartbreak and pain, but the longer I was around Noah the harder that would be.

He was kind, and thoughtful, and saw me. He didn't think of me as an employee. He didn't think I was plain. He seemed interested in me as a person.

That should be enough.

But each day, I wanted more.

I pushed that thought away. It couldn't happen. It wouldn't. We were living in different worlds. We could be friends, but anything more than that was unrealistic.

"The pond's right over here." He led me along the path until he stopped us at a bench overlooking the pond.

It was frozen, covered with a thin layer of snow. The plants around it were dead and there were no cute ducks around. But it was beautiful. Serene.

I scooted closer to him, for warmth of course.

He put his arm around me, it was so easy to let myself melt into him. "See, this is nice."

I nodded and forced myself to think about anything other than how hard his body was. "It is."

He looked around for a minute before facing me. "What do you want to do with your life?"

I chuckled and turned enough to look at him. "What do you mean? I'm already in a career."

He shrugged, looking ahead, not at me. "True. I plan on being a hockey player for as long as I physically can, but that's fifteen, maybe twenty years at most. I don't know what I want to do after that."

I watched him. His focus was somewhere far away. "Well, you could coach or host a show or run a foundation. You could still get a degree if you wanted. You could do anything."

"Maybe you're right. I just never thought past playing. Now I'm here."

"So, enjoy the moment."

He was quiet for a little while. "Do you want children?"

That caught me off guard. "I'm not sure. I guess I always assumed I would, but now that I'm at a point in my life where it's a real possibility, I'm not sure. I couldn't do my job with a child. I'd have to put it in daycare, which is fine. But I worry I would miss out on things."

"Neither of your parents were home, right?"

"No, they both worked."

"Do you feel like you missed out? Or they did?"

I looked down at my hands. "Yeah, but they were pretty good about being there for major things."

"That's what matters."

I nudged him. "What about you? Do you want kids?"

"I think so. At least one."

"How many siblings do you have?"

"Two. An older brother and a younger one."

I smiled. "You're the middle child?"

"Yeah." I could hear the smile in his voice.

"You miss them?"

"I really do. I feel like I'm missing so much of their lives.

We've always been as close as we could be, with the distance, but it's different now that we're older.

"Me too. My sister was my best friend growing up."

"And now?"

"Now she has her own family."

"You miss her."

I was surprised he noticed. "Yeah, I don't see her as much as I'd like."

"Why not?"

"My job is to manage other people's lives. That doesn't give me a lot of time to take vacations or time off. Before that I was in school and didn't have the money to fly home."

"Growing up sucks."

I laughed. "It really does. No one tells you when you're a kid or in school the harsh reality of what life is like."

Not that I would have changed any of my decisions. I loved what I did. I loved my college experience. Growing up was an unavoidable part of life and even though it was hard, and a little bit scary, it was worth it.

He was quiet again, and after a moment I looked up at him to find him watching me. When our eyes connected he smiled.

"You're different from what I expected."

"What do you mean?"

"When Bryce told me I was getting a PA I thought it would be some stuffy guy who was on his phone all the time and ignored me. I wasn't expecting you."

I smiled and looked away. "I wasn't really expecting someone like you either."

"Yeah?"

"Yeah. Bryce told me there was a new player who needed some help. I was expecting some eighteen-year-old punk who would spend all his money in a week. I thought

91

I would have to babysit, you know, more than I already am."

He laughed and squeezed me closer. "Wow. Harsh."

I fell against him with a laugh.

"But I'm not like that?"

"Well, you're more than that." I paused, not knowing if I should tell him what I was thinking. It wasn't exactly within the bounds of a professional relationship. "I think of you as a friend."

I watched for a reaction, but he gave none. He just looked into my eyes. "I think you might be one of my first real friends."

"Really?"

He nodded. "I don't let people in very often, but with you I didn't stand a chance. You bulldozed into my world and planted yourself there."

"Do you mind?" I teased a bit.

"Not at all. I can't picture my life without you now."

"That's just because I buy your food."

He smiled and shook his head. "It's a little bit more than that."

I felt breathless. "Really?"

He nodded and slowly, painfully slow, he lowered his head and tilted my chin up with his hand. Our lips met, and a sudden warmth spread through my body. I sighed and leaned into him, needing to feel closer.

His lips were soft, gentle, but met mine with a passion I hadn't expected.

The sound of cameras filled my ears and I pulled back.

Of course.

How could I have been so stupid? That wasn't real. He was doing it for their benefit.

I turned my head and looked up to keep the tears from

escaping. How could I have forgotten? How did I get so wrapped up in the moment?

I was so stupid.

None of this was real. It was all for show.

"We shouldn't do that." I barely got the words out without my voice cracking.

He leaned forward, trying to meet my eyes, but I looked away. "We shouldn't kiss."

"You're supposed to be my girlfriend. We agreed it was part of the rules. "

This was the worst idea ever. I thought I could fake it. I thought I could go through with this, but I was an idiot. There was more between us than just work. I could feel it. I knew he could too.

Maybe I was lying to myself. Maybe it was all one sided.

"Fine, but at least warn me next time." I stood and started walking back to his building. The stupid cameras were there, waiting. I smiled so they didn't think we'd just fought and waited for Noah to catch up. I couldn't storm off. That would make things look bad, and I wasn't ready to do damage control.

He put his arm around me and continued walking. "I'm sorry, Colby. I promise not to kiss you again without your permission."

I didn't want that. I didn't want to have to tell him when and where it was okay. I wanted to kiss him now, and five minutes from now, and tomorrow. But this wasn't going to work without boundaries.

Kissing him had been the best and worst thing to happen to me. It showed me how much I felt about him, but it reminded me that none of this is real.

I waited until we were close to the front doors before speaking. I didn't want any of the paparazzi to overhear.

"We'll just have to be respectful of each other. I don't want either of us getting hurt."

"Why would we get hurt?" He held the door open for me and I stepped inside.

"Hopefully, we won't." I forced a smiled and walked to the elevator. I really, really hoped we could do this without me breaking.

11

NOAH

I was worried after the day at the park that things between me and Colby would be awkward, but she went on like nothing had happened. Nothing. Like no walk, no moments, no kiss.

She was back to business and I wasn't sure I liked it, but I didn't want to hurt her. That was the last thing I wanted.

I needed to ask her. To make sure we were on the same page, but I didn't know how to bring it up.

I left for practice without seeing her. She normally came by in the mornings, but she left me a message that she was running errands and would be at practice. Even though it seemed valid enough, I felt like she was avoiding me.

There was nothing I could do about it now. I had to push her out of my mind and focus on practice.

After I got to the arena and put on my pads, I was one of the first on the ice. I wanted to warm up a bit since these practices were still killing me.

I was on my second sprint when Coach Rust walked onto the ice and waved me over. I stopped in front of him, feeling a bit of trepidation.

"Morning, Coach."

"Noah, Coach Romney wanted to have a word with you before practice. Would you mind coming with me?"

"Of course." I followed him off the ice and slapped on my blade protectors before walking through the tunnels with him. He didn't give me any hints of what Coach wanted to talk about. No smile or frown. Nothing. His face was completely blank, and I couldn't figure out what that meant. Was I in trouble? Was I getting kicked off the team? My NHL career had lasted one game. That had to be a new record.

He pushed opened the door to the office and gestured for me to enter. I did, and he shut the door behind me.

"Noah, how are you?"

I looked at Coach sitting behind his desk for any sign of his mood. He was too hard to read.

"I'm good, sir."

"Good. Go ahead and take a seat."

I moved in front of one of the chairs and sat down. I rubbed my hands over my thighs and waited.

"I wanted to tell you that we've noticed how much work you're putting in. It hasn't been all smooth, but your dedication has never wavered."

"Thank you, sir." I swallowed and waited for the inevitable 'but'.

"The guys have been talking about you, too."

Oh no. I knew going to dinner with them was a mistake. I ran through that night at fast forward, trying to remember what I could have said or done. Had I offended Madeline somehow?

"They've been impressed with your dedication and the skills you've displayed during practice and the last game."

Wait, this was good news? They liked me?

"Grant sustained a minor sprain yesterday during practice."

My heart stopped beating. He was one of the defensemen from the first line. This wasn't happening.

"We're moving you to the first line."

No. Way. I was starting? I'd be going on with Brassard, Hartman, Murray, and Schultz. There was no way.

"Really?"

I knew I sounded like an inexperienced rookie, but I was. This was amazing. I never would have thought I would get to this point. Not for a few years.

"Yes, Noah. You're going to be practicing with the first line and starting with them in this weekend's game."

I stood and extended my hand. "Thank you, sir. I won't let you down."

He smiled, just a fraction of an inch, but I saw it. "I know you won't. Now get back out there. Practice is starting."

I nodded and walked out of his office feeling like I'd just won the lottery. I was floating. Nothing. Absolutely nothing could be better than this.

I wanted to go to the locker room and send Colby a text. I wanted her to know. I knew she would celebrate with me. She knew how big this was.

I paused. She was the first person I wanted to tell? What about my parents? My old coaches? They were the ones who had been through this journey with me. Why was it that she came to mind first?

I didn't have time to text her. Plus, she would be here. She would see it for herself.

I went out to the bench and took a sip of water. A few more of the guys were out and when I stepped out to the ice, Hartman came over.

"Congratulations, man. Coach told me the news and I'm really happy for you. You deserve it."

"Thanks." I wasn't sure he was entirely correct, but I wasn't going to point it out to him. There were two other defensemen who could have taken this spot. They were older, more experienced, and probably more qualified. But if Coach thought I was the best choice right now, I wasn't going to question it.

"Today's going to be a lot of work, but it will pay off on Saturday."

I nodded and followed him out to warm up.

This was surreal. I was going to be starting with the captain. With my heroes.

I looked around at the empty seats but didn't see Colby yet. I couldn't wait to see her expression when she saw me practicing with these guys.

A whistle blew, and I looked back at the bench. Everyone was out, and Coach was standing in the center. "We've got a game in two days. Today we are going to hit it hard, and tomorrow we'll just be running drills. Malkin will be moving up to the first line for this game, so we'll be rearranging things a little."

A few of the guys looked at me and nodded. I tried to avoid the gaze of the ones who had been skipped over. It wasn't my fault, but I felt a little guilty.

Hartman slapped my back. "Come on, let's do this."

I pushed myself harder than I ever have and when we finally got a break about thirty minutes later, I got a chance to look around. Chloe, Colby, and Emma were sitting in the front row. Colby caught my eye and waved. I nodded back, and she mouthed 'congrats'. She'd figured it out. She knew I was on the first line. Pride washed over me. I was embarrassed by my reaction. I was a grown man, but I felt like a child who had won over the praise of his favorite teacher. I'd done it.

I kept up with the guys and was dead on my feet by the time Coach let us go. I followed the guys to stretch then claimed an ice bath. Every inch of my body was screaming in pain. It was a good thing tomorrow would be a little easier, or I wouldn't be able to move when the game started.

After I showered and dressed, I left the locker room to see Colby waiting. She ran at me and threw her arms around my neck the second I stepped out. I laughed and caught her before we both went to the ground.

"You did it! Noah, I'm so proud of you!"

I squeezed her, soaking in her praise. This felt right. I hadn't liked the distance that had been between us since our date, but this was it. I felt it in my bones. We might have a professional relationship, but this was real. This was how we were supposed to be.

"Thank you."

She released her grip around my neck and backed up. "How are we going to celebrate?"

I bit back a cringe. I wanted to go home and relax. Ice some of my muscles, maybe watch a movie. But she was so excited. I didn't want to let her down.

"Whatever you want."

Her eyes narrowed. "No, this is your day. We're going to do exactly what you want."

"Lunch?"

She tilted her head. "That's it?"

I sighed. I couldn't lie to her. She'd know. "I really would like to relax."

She nodded. "Then I will pick up lunch on the way home and meet you there. Do you need anything? An ice pack? That cooling rub?"

I shook my head. "I have plenty of both."

"Okay, I'll meet you at home then." She smiled and went up on her toes. Her lips grazed my cheek and I nearly grabbed her and pushed her against the wall.

I wanted to kiss her. Right there. "This is a good chance to practice."

"What?" She sounded breathless.

"A celebratory kiss." I turned until our lips were only a breath apart.

"All for appearances?" she said against my lips.

I craved her touch. "Yes."

"No one's watching." She inched closer.

"Even better. Then no one would see if we mess up." I closed my eyes. Praying for her to close the gap.

"I'll see you soon."

I opened my eyes to see her hurrying off in the opposite direction of the elevator. I watched her until she disappeared around a corner, willing the heat in my core to simmer down.

I didn't bother asking where she was going. There were always a hundred things going on in her mind, and I probably couldn't keep up.

By the time I got home, my legs were aching. I went to my room and used a foam roller to loosen the muscles. It was a great mixture of pain and relief. One of those things that hurts so good.

I heard the front door open, so I got up and wandered into the kitchen. Colby was setting two bags on the counter. "What did you get?"

She looked up and smiled at me. "I got you a steak bowl. Don't worry, it's sugar-free, low fat, and low carb."

"Thank you." One day she might stop teasing me about my diet, but I doubted that day would come anytime soon.

She slid the bowl toward me and opened one for herself. "Did you get the same thing?"

She nodded and made a face. "You're a bad influence."

I laughed. "Because you're eating healthy?"

"Yeah. Next you're going to have me exercising."

My eyes roamed over her body involuntarily. She was perfect. Lean without being too skinny. If that was how she looked without worrying about her diet or exercising she was lucky.

"Only if you want to."

She shrugged. "It probably wouldn't hurt." She patted her stomach. "I could probably lose a few pounds."

I stood and walked around the counter to her. I pulled her hands away and held them in mine. "Don't ever say that. You are absolutely perfect the way you are. You're beautiful."

Her eyebrows shot up. I couldn't tell if she believed me or not.

"Your body is amazing." I looked down at her curves, sliding my hands to her waist. "I don't want you to ever think otherwise."

"Really?" Doubt filled her voice.

"I would never lie to you."

She sucked in a breath, bringing my eyes to her lips. They were plump, ready, waiting for mine.

"I'm going to-"

I pressed my lips against hers. I couldn't wait another second. She leaned into me, deepening the kiss and opening her mouth to me. I slid my tongue along her lower lip.

This was so much better than being on the first line.

She jumped back and lifted her hand to her mouth. "Why? Why did you do that?"

I didn't understand why she was upset. That kiss was

amazing. I knew she thought so. Why was she fighting me now?

"I thought..." I smiled but her face was a mix of hurt and worry. I hadn't meant to hurt her. That was the last thing I ever wanted to do. "I'm sorry."

"You shouldn't have done that, Noah."

"Why?"

"There wasn't anyone else here. No cameras. No reporters. Why?"

I shook my head. "I wanted to?"

"Noah." She sighed and turned around and walked out of the room. I heard the guest bedroom door shut a second later.

What just happened? I didn't understand why she was upset. I hadn't meant to hurt her or make her angry. I thought we were having a moment. I saw the way she was looking at me. I thought she wanted it too.

I waited for a minute, hoping she would come back out. When she didn't I went back to my lunch. I didn't know if she wanted me to go after her or give her space. This was our first fight, or misunderstanding. I wasn't sure how to react.

I'd finish, then heat up her lunch and bring it to her. A peace offering was probably a good idea.

A few minutes later, I knocked on her door. "Colby, can I come in?"

I heard a muffled voice, so I took that as a yes.

I opened the door and looked around. She was sitting on the bed, facing away from me. I set her lunch down on the nightstand and sat next to her, careful to leave some space.

"I'm sorry, Colby."

She sighed but didn't look at me.

"I know we agreed to warn each other. I know this is

supposed to be fake. I know I caught you off guard. I'm sorry for all of that."

She turned slightly and briefly met my gaze.

"I'm not sorry for kissing you though."

Her shoulders slumped, and she turned her back to me.

What was I saying wrong? Maybe she didn't see me that way. Maybe she wasn't interested in me.

"I'll try not to do it again. I can't promise it though."

"Why not?"

She was talking to me! I almost stood up and cheered. She probably wouldn't appreciate that though.

"Because you're you."

"What does that mean?"

"It means you're my friend. The person I'm closest to. When I got the news today from Coach that I was moving to the first line, you were the very first person I thought of. It was you who I wanted to tell. You're the most important person in my life."

She shook her head and I stopped. She turned around and her expression nearly broke me. She looked so dejected. "Noah, this isn't real. This is something Bryce came up with. You don't really care about me. I'm just the most convenient. I'm not important to you, I'm just the only one around. Once you get more established here and make more friends, you'll realize I'm nothing more than your personal assistant."

She was wrong. About everything. She would never be just my PA.

I clenched my fist. "You're not listening to me. And stop being so hard on yourself. Don't discount my words and my feelings just because I'm in a new situation. Yeah, I'm young, but you're not that much older than me. A few months doesn't give you a whole life's worth of experience to hold over my head."

She looked at me with... sympathy? "I'm sorry. I'm not trying to tell you how to feel. I'm just trying to prepare myself for the day that you'll no longer need me. This is all temporary. Even if you don't get a contract with the Fury, you'll get picked up by another team. You're talented and people are finally getting to see that. You'll move on. You'll realize you're destined for bigger and better things than me."

I was getting angry now. I hated that she thought of me that way. I wasn't shallow. I wasn't going to get swept up in the fast life. I was trying to tell her what she meant to me and she was blowing me off.

I couldn't sit here and take it anymore.

"I warmed up your lunch for you. I'm going to go watch a movie." I stood and walked out before she could say anything else.

I hated fighting with her. I hated that she was upset, but I wasn't going to sit back and let her tell me how I was supposed to feel. How things were supposed to be. I wasn't following someone else's plans for my life. I didn't care what everyone else was doing. I care about me. Reaching my goals. Being true to myself.

She wasn't willing to hear that though.

12

COLBY

He didn't understand. He didn't get that with each look. Each touch. Each kiss it was breaking my heart even more.

I wanted to leave. I needed to get away, but I couldn't. This was my job. I needed to do this no matter how much it hurt.

Even if I distanced myself from him, I could only do it here. In public I'd have to be the dutiful girlfriend. I could fake it. I would have to, but it would suck.

My phone vibrated next to me on then bed. I checked the screen and was surprised to see my mom's name. She rarely called me outside of our scheduled Sunday calls. But maybe she remembered.

"Hi Mom."

"Hi, honey. I'm surprised I caught you."

"Yeah, what's up?" I waited for her to say 'happy birthday' or for Dad to jump on the line.

"I just wanted to let you know that your father and I have made an important decision."

I could tell by her tone that she wasn't calling with good news. Dread washed over me. Could this day really get worse? The possibilities ran through my mind. Was one of them sick? Were they getting a divorce?

"What's going on Mom?"

"We're selling the house."

That was probably the last thing I expected. "But you love that house. You've lived there for over thirty years."

She sighed. "I know, dear. There are a lot of memories here, but we decided to take advantage of the market and sell."

My childhood home. The only place I'd ever lived growing up. I moved around to different apartments in college, but that was my home. My safe place. That was where I learned to ride a bike. I'd had my first boys and girls party in the backyard. I got my first kiss in the driveway. Everything happened in that house.

I took a breath. This wasn't about me. This was their decision. I was an adult with my own place. I couldn't expect them to stay there forever. "Where are you moving?"

"We're actually going to travel for a little while."

This was getting weirder and weirder. "So, you're selling the house and traveling?"

"Yeah, we're going to start in Mexico, then work our way through Central and South America, then Australia, and Asia and end in Europe."

What the heck was happening? Who was this person? My parents were safe. Stable. They would never, ever pick up and travel the world.

I tried to be happy for them. This was their time. Their golden years. "That sounds amazing, Mom."

"Oh, thank you, honey. We're very excited, but we were

worried about you. We didn't want you to feel like we were leaving you out."

I instantly felt guilty. They worried about telling me? They expected me to be upset. What kind of daughter did that make me? I wasn't so selfish that I'd be mad at them for pursuing a dream. They'd always supported me. I hated that they didn't think I would support them.

"I'm really happy for you guys, this will be a really great experience for you."

We talked for a few more minutes before hanging up. I tried to control my voice. Not letting her know I was upset. I had no reason to be. It was their house. They were free to do with it whatever they wanted. I couldn't get upset about them moving on with their lives. They were empty nesters. They were free to travel and see the world. It was a dream my mom had talked about when I was a child, but I never thought they would go through with it.

The realization that she'd forgotten my birthday sunk in. Through our whole conversation she didn't once mention it. Never even hinted. How could she forget? She never had before. Getting the house ready to sell must be stressful. Her mind was probably on other things.

I looked at my food and scowled. It was no longer appealing.

I didn't want to eat. Or think too much about anything.

I picked it up and went back into the kitchen. After putting it in the fridge I looked into the living room. I couldn't see Noah's head, so he must be lying down. I didn't recognize the movie he was watching. Something with fancy cars and a lot of guns.

I walked over and peeked over the couch. His head was on a pillow, facing the TV.

"Hey."

He looked up at me and smiled. "Hi."

"Can I sit with you?"

"Of course."

He started to sit up, but I stopped him. "I'm just going to go right here." I moved to his feet and lifted them up, then sat and put them on my lap.

"I can move." He pulled his knees up, but I put my hand on them and pulled them back down.

"No, you're fine."

He set his head back on the pillow and we watched in silence for a few minutes.

"Who was on the phone?"

I looked over at him, but he was focused on the movie.

"My mom."

"Anything exciting going on back home?"

I chuckled. "Just them selling the house and going on a trip around the world."

His head popped up. "Seriously?"

I nodded.

"Are you okay with that?"

"Honestly? Not really. I mean, I get that it's their house and they're free to do whatever they want with it, but it's my childhood home. It's where I grew up. It's the only home I've ever known."

He nodded. "I would be mad if my parents sold ours."

"I guess I thought it would always be there. Even though I haven't been back much since I came here for school, I thought I could always go home."

He smiled sweetly. It was hard to feel too sad when he looked at me with those baby blues. "I think this is where I'm supposed to say home is where the heart is or something like that."

I laughed. "Please don't."

He laughed with me. "I won't."

I leaned my head back against the sofa when he quieted. "I'm sorry, Colby."

I turned my head toward him and smiled. "Me too."

"You're not still mad at me?"

I shook my head.

He raised an eyebrow and grinned. "So, I can kiss you again?"

I kept shaking my head and tried to look stern but ended up laughing. When I calmed down I sighed. "You know the worst part?"

He propped himself up on his elbow and waited.

"She didn't even tell me happy birthday."

His jaw dropped. "Wait. Today's your birthday?"

I nodded.

"Why didn't you tell me sooner? Like last week?"

I shrugged. "I don't normally make a big deal about it, but when my mom called I thought for sure that's why." I chuckled. "Nope, it was just to tell me she was selling my childhood to the highest bidder."

He dropped his legs from my lap and sat up. "Colby, I'm so sorry."

I tried to pretend I was fine, but the second his arm wrapped around my shoulder, I was done. Tears fell, and I turned into him.

He rubbed my back and held me close.

"Happy Birthday, Colby."

I took a breath and looked up at him. "Thank you."

I thought he was going to kiss me. His eyes went to my lips and I leaned forward, just a bit, but he didn't. He was honoring my wishes. He kissed my forehead and pulled me against him again.

"What do you want to do for your birthday?"

I sniffed. "Nothing."

He smiled and nodded once. "Come on."

He laid back down, bringing me with him. He held me against his chest, with me facing the TV. I snuggled back into him. Needing to feel him close to me. I know I was going against everything I'd told him, but right now I just needed him. To know he was there.

We watched the rest of the movie in silence and when he changed it to a new one with the remote, I fell asleep in his arms.

When I woke up, I was alone in the living room. I sat up and looked around. Great. My mom forgot my birthday and Noah ditched me. He probably saw my teary, snotty face and ran.

I walked back to the guestroom room and went into the bathroom to wash my face. I was grateful I'd had the thought to stash some of my things here. My eyes were a little puffy, but definitely not as bad as what I was expecting. Afterward, I brushed my hair and took a deep breath. No more pity parties. No more tears. I had nothing to be sad about. I had a home. I had food. I had friends. I had much more than most. I couldn't let one stupid day make me sad.

I was finally hungry and couldn't stop thinking about my steak bowl waiting for me in the fridge. As long as Noah didn't eat it while I was sleeping. He wouldn't. Would he?

Maybe that was another rule I had to establish.

My worrying was for nothing. It was sitting right where I left it. I put it in the microwave and leaned against the counter.

I heard a distant vibrating noise and realized I left my phone on the couch. I hurried over to answer. It was Chloe.

"Hi."

"Hey girl. I'm coming to get you."

I looked down at myself. I wasn't in a going out mood. And I didn't look ready. "Oh Chloe, that's really nice but I'm not- "

"This isn't optional. Don't worry about getting ready. I have something for you. Just open the door for me."

I sighed. There was no stopping her. I knew that already.

"Fine, just let me know when you're here."

"I'm here."

I turned and looked at the door. "At Noah's place?"

"Yup. Now hurry and open the door, my arms are going to fall off."

I hurried to the door and opened it. She burst in with arms full of bags. I could barely see her face. I had no idea how she was able to call me until I saw Madeline walking in behind, still holding the phone.

"What are you guys doing here?" I probably looked horrible and puffy. The last thing I needed was seeing them both perfectly put together and polished. I felt like a troll next to them.

"We're here to get you ready." Madeline took my hand and led me to the guestroom without hesitation.

"Ready for what?" My head was spinning. Why were they here and where was Noah?

"We're going out." That was all she told me before Chloe walked in and dropped all of the bags on the guest bed.

"It's going to take all of those to get me ready?" I cringed. I didn't think I looked that bad on a daily basis but with all of that I could only assume they were on a mission for a full makeover.

"Oh these? No, this is for all of us." Chloe started sorting through them while Madeline pulled me into the bathroom.

"Sit."

I looked at her through the mirror. There wasn't a chair. I didn't understand what she wanted me to do. "On the floor?"

She blinked and looked around. "Dang it. In my head this went like a movie. You'd have a vanity and I'd sit you down and play with your hair before finding inspiration and making you look like a vixen."

I laughed and went back to the room. I grabbed the chair at the desk and brought It back to the bathroom.

"Perfect. Okay, sit down."

I followed her instruction and she played with my hair, pushing it all forward and shaping it around my shoulders. "Alright. I know what I'm going to do."

"You're not cutting it, right?"

Her eyes got wide. "Oh heavens no. I wouldn't do that to you. I'm just going to curl it."

I relaxed and sat back. "Okay good."

"Geez don't sound too relieved. You're ruining this moment for me."

She smirked, and I couldn't help but giggle. "Sorry I didn't realize this was so important to you."

She stared at me through the mirror. "It's my first time doing an intervention."

"This is an intervention? From what?"

"From your pity party." Chloe walked in carrying a garment bag. "Noah let us know you needed a fun night out, so here we are."

I narrowed my eyes. "That's all he said?"

She nodded and walked back into the bedroom. She returned a second later with a box. She set it down on the counter and I realized it was a three-drawer storage container, filled with makeup. Good grief.

Madeline put her hands on my shoulder and squeezed once. "Shower really quick and we'll get started."

She and Chloe disappeared while I took a record-breaking shower. The second I was out and decently covered, they were back.

Chloe clapped once. "Let's get to work."

Madeline curled my hair into tight spirals while Chloe stood in front of me, blocking my view of the mirror. She used more makeup on my face than I'd use in a week.

Thirty minutes later, they both stepped away and I saw my reflection. I gasped and touched my hair. My normally straight locks were flowing over my shoulders in luscious waves.

"How did you do this?" I'd never been able to get my hair to curl, let alone look like this.

Madeline shrugged. "Practice."

I looked back at my reflection. Chloe had done a smokey eye and nude lip. I looked good. Sexy even.

"Wow you guys. You're both so amazing."

Chloe shrugged it off. "When we try we can look pretty good."

Madeline laughed. "Yeah, it's fun to get all dolled up. I live in a ponytail at work, so I like to get fancy sometimes."

I looked at each of them. Chloe's hair was wavy, as it normally was, and she didn't have a lot of makeup on. Madeline's hair was curled, but it didn't look like she was getting ready to go out either.

"What about you guys?"

"We'll fix ourselves while you get dressed." She pointed to the white garment bag hanging on the shower door.

I took it and walked into the closet. There was no point in trying to argue. They were women on a mission.

I unzipped the bag and caught a glimpse of dark purple.

A rich plum. I pushed back the sides of the bag to reveal the dress. It looked like it would hit my knees and it had cap sleeves. I undressed and pulled it off the hanger to slip it on. I reached back to pull up the zipper and gasped. The front had a see-through panel down the center that went up to the shoulders. Everything that needed to be covered was, but it was far more revealing than anything I'd ever worn.

I opened the door and Madeline turned with a mascara wand held up near her eye. Chloe was curling a piece of hair but dropped it when she saw me.

"You look amazing!" She hurried forward and forced to me spin. She pulled the zipper all the way up then turned me back around to face her. "You need to take off the bra, Colby."

I clenched my jaw. "I'm not wearing this."

Madeline turned to face me with a worried look. "Why not?"

"It's too much. I can't go out like this." I crossed my arms over my chest, trying to cover my exposed bits.

"But Colby, you look absolutely amazing." She and Chloe were looking me over, head to toe.

"Madi's right. This is perfect."

I shook my head. "I can't."

"Why not? You look so great. This dress was made for you."

"I feel half naked. One wrong move and I'll be showing all my goods."

Madeline laughed while Chloe shook her head. "Oh honey. You look beautiful, but if you don't love it you can wear the backup." She disappeared into the room and came back with another garment bag. "Try this."

I looked to Madeline for help, but she just nodded. I sighed and turned around. I stepped out of the dress and hung it up before unzipping the new option. It was a silver, flapper style dress.

I couldn't stop smiling the second I slipped it on. No cleavage. No cutout. I twisted my hips and laughed as the fringe danced around me.

I emerged from the closet and they both squealed. Like young girls.

"You look amazing!" Chloe was beaming at me like she was my fairy godmother.

"It's perfect. Absolutely perfect." Madeline stepped forward and grabbed my shoulders, moving me until I was staring at my reflection. She played with my hair, ruffling the roots and bringing my curls forward. "You're stunning."

I resisted the urge to roll my eyes and looked in the mirror. The dress wasn't something I'd ever pick on my own, but I couldn't help admiring how I looked in it. I felt mature. Maybe even a little sexy.

"You guys don't think it's too much?"

They shook their heads simultaneously.

"Give us a second to change, then we'll get going." Chloe pulled Madeline's hand and they disappeared into the bedroom.

I ran my hands over the front of the dress, then turned to the side. It was really flattering. I went back to my closet and slipped on some black peep toe heels.

"Ready, Colby?" Madeline was standing by the door looking absolutely stunning in a cream, column dress. It had a slit up the thigh but covered much more than mine.

"Yeah, let's go."

Chloe handed me a small clutch that matched my dress. I looked inside and found my phone, keys, and lipstick. How did she get all that without me knowing?

"This is going to be so much fun." She walked ahead of us, calling the elevator before I even had the door locked.

"Where are we going?"

"Don't worry about that." Madeline winked. Normally, I would demand more answers but at this point I was just along for the ride. They hadn't let me down so far.

13

NOAH

Everyone around me was enjoying themselves, talking, laughing, not silently freaking out like I was. I didn't know if this was a good idea. It had seemed like it a few hours ago. Chloe had assured me it was brilliant, but I wasn't so sure.

I knew Colby needed cheering up. I wanted to celebrate her and make her happy again. I just wished I knew if this was something she'd enjoy. I felt like a jerk for not knowing. She probably knew my idea of a good time. She was better at paying attention to details.

I looked around the darkened room, the private floor of a swanky restaurant downtown, where all of the team and their significant others were gathered.

Once I called Chloe, she told me not to worry about anything. All I had to do was look nice and be ready at eight. I checked my watch for the hundredth time. It was three minutes till. They should be here any minute. My phone vibrated in my pocket. I pulled it out to see a message from Chloe. They were parking.

"Alright guys! They're parking. They'll be here any second."

To my surprise, people listened to me. Someone dimmed the lights even lower and people moved to the shadows. I moved to the front of the room and waited for the door to open. It was silent, and I was so grateful everyone was taking this seriously. This was a big deal for me, and for Colby.

I heard a door open above us, then footsteps down the stairs. Any second now.

The entry door swung open and the second I saw her honey brown hair I jumped out and yelled surprise with everyone else.

Colby jumped back, with her hand on her chest, and was caught by Madeline.

Someone turned on more lights and Chloe and Madeline moved Colby forward.

"Oh my gosh!" Colby stepped forward, her eyes sweeping over the room before settling on me. She stepped forward until she was standing in front of me. "You did this?"

I nodded. "Happy Birthday."

She threw her arms around me and I stumbled a bit before catching myself and hugged her. "Thank you."

When she finally released me, I got a chance to really look at her, and I knew stopping was going to be a problem.

"You look gorgeous." She really did. Looked flawless. Her dress made her look like she just walked out of a movie. I could stare at her all night, but this party wasn't for me. This was all about celebrating her. I'd been surprised when all the guys showed up. I didn't think everyone would come, especially since it was me asking. Well, Chloe asked, but on my behalf.

Colby squeezed my hand. "Thanks, Noah. Thanks for doing all of this. I was planning on spending the night eating ice cream and feeling sad for myself."

"I couldn't let that happen. Not on your twenty-first birthday."

She smiled and gave me another hug before stepping back and looking around. "This place is amazing. So chic."

It was a cool restaurant. I didn't know how Chloe reserved it on such short notice, probably a perk of her job. She knew the right people and could always call in a favor.

"Let's go take a look around." I said while she looked around.

She smiled up at me and slid her hand into mine. It felt natural, but I couldn't tell if this was for us, or for show. Right now, it didn't matter. I wanted her to have a great night, but I also wished I could have her to myself. She looked like a dream in her vintage dress. I didn't like feeling the eyes from every single guy in the room gravitating to her. I couldn't ruin this for her, though. I wanted her to feel like a part of the team, like the other women in the Pride.

I introduced her to each guy and they told her happy birthday. I expected her to be star struck or overwhelmed but she fit right in. Chloe pulled me away about an hour later. I felt bad leaving Colby alone, but Emma and Olli stepped in and started talking to her.

"We have her cake ready. Do you want to jump out of it?"

I stared at her. She couldn't be serious.

She broke out laughing and held up her hand. "Oh my gosh, I wish you could see your face right now." She kept laughing while I took a breath and tried to get my heart rate down.

She turned and led me to the kitchen where a normal sized cake was waiting. It was three-tiered with white frosting and decorated with red flowers, mini black pucks and sticks.

"You got her a hockey cake?"

Chloe was beaming. "Isn't it perfect?"

I shook my head. "Why?"

She swatted my arm. "I got an even more childish one for Madi's birthday and she loved it. Trust me. This is going to be a hit."

I didn't have any other options than to trust her. "Okay."

She handed me a lighter and I lit the twenty-two candles before we walked the cart to the main room. Madeline was standing at the door and dimmed the lights when we got close. The roomful of people started singing Happy Birthday with Colby standing in the center. She started laughing when she saw the cake but looked genuinely happy. I guess Chloe knew what she was doing. Yet again.

When the singing ended, Colby stepped forward and blew out all the candles while everyone cheered around her. She looked up at me, happier than I'd ever seen her. She mouthed thank you as Chloe pushed forward and began removing the candles. A restaurant employee slid by and began cutting the cake.

"Wait I want a picture of it!" Colby looked around. "Where's my bag?"

"I'll take it." I took my phone out of my pocket and took a few shots before Colby nodded, looking appeased.

"I got a video of the singing and blowing out the candles." Chloe told Colby over her shoulder. Of course, she did. The woman was like super girl.

The waiters came out and began serving the cake while people began dispersing and talking again. Colby was surrounded by people. I was amazed at how quickly she became part of the group. I wasn't going to flatter myself and think it was because of me. I was just as new. No, people seemed to gravitate toward her. It was her persona, charisma. She seemed lonely when I first met her, but maybe it was because she hadn't found her people. Right now, it looked like she had.

I gave her space throughout the night. I didn't want to hover, even though I wanted to be right next to her. She was smiling and laughing. All that mattered was that she was happy and having a good time.

It was crazy to think we'd only known each other for a couple of weeks. She was such an integral part of my life now. I couldn't imagine a day without her.

What was that? Was that just me appreciating her? She did so much for me. So many things I'm sure went unnoticed. Being around her was natural. As easy as breathing. But did that just mean we were compatible? Good friends?

Now wasn't the best time to analyze my feelings. Surrounded by my teammates and new friends.

"There you are." I looked over my shoulder to where Madeline was walking toward me.

"Hey." I was sitting at the bar, facing the group. It wasn't like I was hiding in the corner.

"Colby's been asking where you are."

I looked to the center of the room where she was chatting with Hartman and a woman I didn't recognize. "She looks like she's having a good time."

"She is."

I felt her eyes on me but didn't look.

"It's really sweet that you did this," she said.

I shrugged. "I was just trying to do something nice for her."

"This is a little above and beyond something nice for

your personal assistant. I'm not sure anyone else here has ever thrown a birthday party for theirs."

She was probably right. I knew this wasn't normal. But she wasn't just my PA. She was my friend.

"What are you getting at, Madeline?"

I finally turned to her to see her smile. "You can call me Madi. We're friends now."

I nodded.

"I just think there's something more to this than a nice gesture for a PA."

"She's also my friend."

"And your girlfriend I hear."

I rolled my eyes. Most of the guys knew it was Bryce's idea. It had been Colby's idea to let the team know the truth, in case we slipped. I could trust them not to go to the press about it.

"You know that's fake."

She smirked. "Is it?" She held up her phone. A picture of me and Colby walking through the park was on the screen. We were holding hands and looking at each other like we were completely in love.

"Trick of the camera."

Her smirk turned into a full-blown grin. "Oh Noah. Don't be an idiot. There's photographic evidence that there's more between you two than business or even friendship."

"A single picture doesn't prove that."

"Oh really?" She scrolled through the page, revealing more and more images of us together. Us drinking our hot chocolate. Us sitting on the bench, arms wrapped around each other. Me standing in front of her when she was freaking out about going to the aviary. It was obvious. I could see my feelings clearly, but how did she feel about me?

122

I sighed and leaned back against the bar. "What do you want me to say, Madi?"

"I want you to admit there's more to these than a fake relationship."

"I can't do that. Things are new. We're still getting to know each other. I think I know how I feel, but I'm not sure about Colby."

She clapped and threw her fist in the air like she'd just won a game. "I knew it."

I began to panic. Was this a set up? Did she have a mic on?

"You and Colby are our new mission."

"What? What do you mean 'our'?"

She waved and suddenly Chloe appeared. Oh crap. They're in on this together.

"Did he admit it?"

Madi nodded. "Now we just need her to."

I held up my hands. The evil twins needed to be stopped. Where were Reese and Erik when I needed them?

"What are you guys doing? Leave it alone. I'll be the one to figure out if she feels the same about me. I don't need you two running around trying to play matchmaker."

Chloe scoffed. "I can't believe you think so lowly of us. We're not matchmaking."

Madi giggled. "Yeah, we'll keep to ourselves."

They looked at each other and laughed as they hurried away. Those two were trouble. I had a bad feeling about whatever they were going to do.

I tried to forget about them and made my way through the crowd to Colby. When I got close she noticed me and reached out her arm. I took her hand and pulled her close to me. "Are you having fun?"

She nodded. "Thank you so much for this."

I thought she might let my hand go and find another group to talk to, but she moved closer. She rested her head on my arm, not quite tall enough to reach my shoulder, and chatted with the people around us.

Brassard walked up to us and raised an eyebrow when he saw her leaning on me. "Happy Birthday, Colby."

"Thank you." She smiled at him but made no move. I was a little relieved. I knew I shouldn't be self-conscious, but it was hard around these guys. They were all older, more experienced, better players, richer, and probably more attractive. It was hard being around them, especially when Colby looked as amazing as she did. I wouldn't be surprised if one of the single guys swept her off her feet right out from under me.

"I'm heading out, but you guys have fun." He winked and disappeared in the crowd.

"Is it late?" Colby looked up at me.

I checked my watched and answered her. "It's eleven."

Erik and Madi took his spot and I shot a warning look to her. She just smiled back at me.

"Brassard has been mopey for years. I'm surprised he even came." Erik put his arm around Madi. "Hasn't been the same since Lucy."

"Who's Lucy?" I was wondering the same thing, but grateful Colby had been the one to say it.

"An old ghost." Erik brushed off the question. "We're heading out. Got to rest up for the game."

We said our goodbyes and I realized that was probably a good idea for me too. I didn't want to end Colby's night early though. Maybe I could make sure she had a ride with someone else.

I looked over when she leaned her head on me again, yawning.

"Are you tired?"

She looked up at me, lazily. "A bit."

"Do you want to make the rounds then head home?"

She nodded and followed me around the room. We said goodbye, they told her happy birthday. She was smiling the whole time. I'd been worried before she got here that she wouldn't enjoy it. I didn't know yet if she liked parties, but it looked like I made the right choice.

After we were in the car and headed to her house she sighed. "Thanks again for tonight, Noah. That was the best birthday I've ever had."

"Even with all the crap from earlier?"

She looked at me and smiled. "You made me forget all that."

"Good." I turned onto her street. "You deserve to be celebrated and I wanted you to see how many people love and care about you."

She laughed. "I'm pretty sure most of them didn't know who I was before tonight, but you're right, I felt like I made fifty new friends."

By the time we got to the front door, Colby was leaning on me heavily. "Do you want me to carry you to bed?" I was holding her up by her shoulders, but her eyes were mostly closed.

"No. I'm fine." She took a wobbly step in and I decided it was probably easier, and faster, if I just carried her. I locked the door behind us before putting an arm around her back and under her knees. I swept her up and she yipped before giggling.

"I wasn't expecting that."

"No worries, sleepy head. I'll get you to bed." I walked the short distance to her room wishing it were a mile long. I didn't want to put her down. I didn't want to be farther from her. Being this close to her felt amazing, almost as good as when she was sleeping in my arms on the couch.

I set her down and watched as she fell back, onto the bed. I slid off her heels and set them on the floor. "Do you want to change?"

She grunted but didn't move.

"Maybe wash your face?"

She grunted again.

Alright then. I pulled a blanket off the end of the bed and laid it over her. If she wanted to get up later she could.

I backed out of the room and turned off her light. "Goodnight, Colby."

"Noah?" Her sleepy voice called out to me.

I closed the distance to her bed in three steps. "Yeah?"

I leaned over her and she smiled. "Thank you."

Her arm reached out and her hand landed on my cheek. She rose up and my heart exploded. This was it.

She met my eyes for a split second before leaning forward.

I was frozen. Too scared that any movement would ruin this moment.

I closed my eyes as the space between us shrunk.

Her lips pressed against the corner of my mouth. Not quite my cheek and not quite my lips. I opened my eyes to see her lay back with a sweet smile.

I blew out a breath and stepped back. I stopped at her door waiting to see if she would call out again, but all I heard was her soft snore in response.

14

COLBY

When I woke up I stared at my ceiling. That had to be a dream. My Cinderella-worthy night couldn't have been real. I didn't have fairy godmothers that came and dressed me. I didn't spend the night with the entire Fury team. They didn't get me a custom cake. I didn't have that many people who cared about me.

It was a dream.

I sat up, realizing I wasn't under my sheets. I was on top of the duvet with a throw blanket over me. I looked down and realized I was still in the party dress.

It was real?

I slid off the side of my bed and into my bathroom. I groaned when I saw my reflection. Makeup was smeared everywhere. My eyeliner that had been expertly applied by Chloe was halfway down my face. My curls were limp and sad.

I turned on the shower and stepped out of my magical dress. I swear it was good luck. Last night had been one of the best in my life. Wait. No. I couldn't remember a happier time. It had been the very best.

All thanks to Noah.

When I'd woken up yesterday to an empty apartment I never in a million years would have guessed what he was up to. He treated me better than anyone in my life.

After showering, I dressed in jeans and a comfy t-shirt. It was game day, so I didn't know if Noah would still be around. Normally, he'd be gone for practice by now. I hurried to his apartment and let myself in.

I trudged into the kitchen to see him standing in front of the stove, shirtless.

I gasped, and he turned to me with a smile. "Morning, sunshine."

My eyes would not cooperate. I told them repeatedly to look away from his naked chest, but every time they looked away for a split second they were pulled back. His shoulders, his chest, holy crap his abs. Those things couldn't be real.

I stepped forward but stopped when I realized my hands were reaching to touch him. I needed to leave. Run far away before I completely embarrassed myself. I closed my eyes. "Morning."

"I'm making eggs, want some?"

"Sure."

"Are you going to stand with your eyes closed all day?"

Crap. He noticed. I opened them to see him staring at me with a raised brow. Yeah, I know I look like a crazy person. "Sorry."

"Headache?"

"Sure." We can go with that.

"There's ibuprofen in the cabinet." He lifted an arm to point and it just made all the muscles in his back flex. I groaned and looked at the floor.

"Are you okay?" He asked sounding concerned.

"No."

His bare feet appeared in my line of sight. I slowly looked up his body, stopping when I reached the deep v lines and ripple of abs.

In the name of all that is holy...

I needed to run. Through the window. The snow would cool me down.

"What's wrong?"

I finally met his eyes. They were so clear. So, piercing. Like he could see into my soul.

His lips slowly twisted into a grin. "Is my presence having a negative effect on you?"

I blinked and looked away. "I'm fine."

He stepped away with a laugh and dished up the eggs. He set two plates at the bar. I went to the fridge and stuck my head in. Oh, nice and cold.

"Do you want something to drink? Milk, water, orange juice, a shirt." I whispered the last part hoping he wouldn't hear.

"What was that last option?"

"Sprite?"

He pressed against me, looking in the fridge. "We have soda?"

I closed my eyes. For the love of all that is good. No stomach should be that hard. Arms shouldn't be that large.

I cleared my throat. "Oh no. I thought the lime juice was a bottle."

He laughed, and I prayed he believed me. The last thing that we needed was for him to know about my attraction.

"I'll just have water."

"Good choice." I filled two glasses and set them in front of the plates while he took a seat.

After a second of me staring at the counter he waved. "Are you going to join me?"

That would be the next logical step. He had made me breakfast and when we ate together, we sat here. He was usually clothed.

Could I be that close to him?

Totally. Yeah. I could handle this.

I walked around the counter and sat on the stool. I ate in silence while Noah listened to some sports network on the TV.

"Noah Malkin was seen once again with his girlfriend." I cringed and turned. There was a video of us leaving the party last night. He had his arm around me and I was looking up at him like he hung the moon, stars, and sun. Well, that ought to convince the public we were real. I looked like a lovesick puppy.

The reporter went on to talk about Noah being on the first line today and the predictions for the game. Soon, my face was off the screen and I turned back around to pick at my food.

"That was pretty weird." He sat down his fork.

I nodded.

"I didn't even see them last night."

I hadn't either. "I think that's what they're good at these days."

"I still don't get why they're interested in me."

I looked over at him, from his hair down to his waist. "Yeah, I can't imagine why anyone would find you interesting."

He laughed and looked at me like he had last night. Like he was seeing something. Something more than just my makeup free face and wet hair.

"When do you leave?" I wanted to distract him. Take the

attention off me. I knew the answer. I'd been the one to tell him, but we could pretend like my entire existence didn't revolve around him.

"At ten."

I nodded. He would need to leave soon. "Do you have everything packed?"

"Yeah, it's just a small overnight bag."

"Your itinerary and tickets are in your email."

"Thanks."

We fell back into silence while he finished eating.

"I wish you could come tonight."

I stood with my plate and walked around to the sink. "I wish I could be there too. Dang Coach for making up his mind just two days before."

He smiled and sat back. I took his empty plate and rinsed it off before loading the dishes into the dishwasher.

"I'll be at the next one, and you'll start then too."

He didn't look as confident as I felt about that. "If I don't mess up this game."

He came around into the kitchen and I grabbed his arm with my wet hands. "We've had this talk. You are an amazing player, Noah. You've already proven that. Once you get out there all of your doubts and all the noise will disappear. You're going to kill it tonight."

He looked into my eyes, and I focused on not letting my gaze drop. No matter how badly I wanted to look.

"You really think so?"

I laughed. "Yes, Noah. I know it."

"Thanks." He bent down, and I froze in place. As his lips got closer I inhaled. I was ready for this. I could do this. I tilted my head up, just a bit, as his lips landed on my forehead. He planted one kiss then stepped back, smiling. "I'm going to get dressed."

I watched him walk out wanting to punch him. How could he do that? Make a move and then kiss me. On. The. Forehead.

Like I was a child.

I was fuming. Until I saw my reflection in the window.

He was a professional athlete with the news and media circus following him. He was a star. At this point he really could have any woman he wanted. He should be with someone flawless. Someone refined. Someone he could show off around town.

I wasn't that girl.

I was just his personal assistant.

I was here to make sure he was on time for his flights. I did his grocery shopping and cleaned his apartment. I was around for when he needed a different suit brought to a photoshoot. I was the paid help.

I was practically his wife. I took care of everything, without really being a part of his life.

The realization was a slap to the face. As much as I wanted to pretend like last night was real, our connection was real, it wasn't. It was all pretend.

That was fine.

I rolled my shoulders and went to the living room with my phone to check on emails. I couldn't begrudge him for who he was. That didn't change the fact that I cared for him.

I thought of all he'd done for me last night. As good looking as he was, he was an even better person.

I needed to show him my gratitude. How much I appreciated him.

But how?

He was pretty simple. Didn't have expensive tastes, yet. It wasn't like I could afford to buy him much anyway.

What could I do to show him? Something as brilliant as

the birthday he'd given me?

A few ideas came to me, but there was a limit to what I could pull off. Good thing I knew exactly who could help.

I was going to Emma's house with the rest of the Pride who were in town to watch the game. A lot of the wives were going to the game since it was so close, but the rest of us were getting together.

They would have ideas. Probably better than anything I could come up with on my own.

I went out just as Noah was getting ready to leave.

"You're off?" I asked, stopping him.

He nodded, still looking nervous.

I walked up to him and wrapped my arms around his torso. I almost pulled back. I shouldn't be touching him like this. At least not without cameras. But it felt too good. He was too warm. Too inviting.

When his arms settled around me I sighed. "You're going to be so great. And I'll be watching."

He hugged me back for a moment before stepping back. "Thanks, Colby. I'll call you later."

"Okay." I waved as he walked out the door. I really did wish I were going with him. It might be conceited of me to think I make a difference, but I knew it mattered to him.

Maybe that's what I could do.

I could show up to the game!

I pulled out my phone and called Chloe. If there was any way to make this work, she would know how.

"Hi love." She answered after the first ring.

"Hey, I want to surprise Noah."

She laughed. "What kind of surprise?"

"I want to go to the game tonight."

There was a pause. "Why?"

"It's his first game on the first line and he's really

nervous. I think it would help if he knew I was there."

"Aw. That's sweet."

"So, you'll help me?"

She sighed. "Sorry, girl. I've already tried to get tickets."

"You have?" I thought she could do anything when it came to the team.

"Yeah, when Erik told me Noah got called up to the first line. I thought it would be fun for us to go support him, but tickets were sold out and Denver isn't the nicest to work with. I contacted their front office and they said they couldn't help us. Don't worry, I'll remember this next time they need something."

My hope deflated. "Dang. I thought I had the perfect idea."

"You did, we were just too late."

"Crap. I want to do something for him. Something as awesome as what he did for me."

"Let me think. I'll have some ideas by tonight."

"Okay, thanks. I'll see you later."

I knew I shouldn't have gotten my hopes up. It wasn't like it was a home game. We didn't have any pull when they were away. That just would have been the perfect thing.

Oh well. Between all of us women, we'd come up with something awesome.

I ran errands for the rest of the day before arriving at Emma's house with bags full of chips and dip and salsa.

Emma's house was beautiful. Absolutely perfect, just like her and Olli. Of course.

I let myself in, like she'd told me to do. I could hear laughs from deep in the house. I followed it until I saw them gathered in the kitchen.

"Hey." I walked in, holding out my bags. "I brought junk food."

"Perfect!" Madi grabbed the bags and added them to the impressive spread. There was a fruit and veggie tray, but they were shoved off to the side. The center had two huge trays of street tacos and nachos.

"Oh, this looks so good."

Emma gave me a hug and looked down. "Don't tell the guys this is what we eat when they're gone."

I laughed along with the rest of the women. I knew what they were worried about. The guys were on strict diets, eating clean and rarely cheating. They would have to pass on most of this food. It was too bad for them.

Chloe walked in a minute later with a bottle of wine in each hand. "No men!"

The women cheered, and Emma took a bottle and immediately removed the cork. Soon, glasses were being passed around and I heard a few sighs.

"We're so deprived." Sophia sighed and leaned against the counter with her glass.

"It's a hard knock life for sure." Chloe sipped her wine and smiled.

Emma offered me a glass but I felt a bit guilty. "You can't drink any."

She opened the fridge and pulled out another bottle. "Sparkling cider for me!"

"Oh. I'll take some of that, too."

"Pour some for me!" A few other women joined in and I felt better about not drinking the wine.

We made plates stuffed full of empty calories and sat around the kitchen chatting.

"Madi, what's the latest with the wedding plans?" I leaned forward to see Madi smile at a pretty brunette I'd met last night. I couldn't remember her name though. Jen, maybe?

"The date, venue, and food are all set."

"So, what's left?"

Madi smiled. "Just the dress."

Chloe laughed. "She's seriously the pickiest person I've ever met."

"I am not."

"You've tried on over two hundred dresses."

My jaw dropped along with most of the other women. Madi blushed. "I just can't find what I'm looking for."

Emma laughed. "How about you Chloe?"

"Oh, she's done of course." Madi rolled her eyes and stuffed half a taco in her mouth. I laughed and looked back to Chloe.

She was all smiles. "Everything's coming together. We just need the day to get here."

"When are you getting married?" I didn't want to insert myself like I expected to be included, but I was curious.

"July fifteenth."

"And you, Madi?"

"August third."

"Aw, no double wedding."

Chloe shook her head. "No, this is one thing me and my twin will not share."

Everyone laughed, and we continued eating. I was jealous of them. They'd both found their person. I couldn't imagine how that would feel. To know your future and be confident in it.

Chloe clapped. "Oh! You guys! We have to come up with a surprise for Noah."

The group seemed to perk up. "What kind of surprise?" Emma asked, what I was sure everyone was thinking.

I felt a little self-conscious about this. "I want to do something to thank him for last night."

There were nods and a few mumbles, but no one spoke up.

"I wanted to show up at the game tonight, but it was too late."

Chloe stood up. "I was thinking you could throw a party for him, but that's not as original as what he did for you."

I nodded and waited for someone else to come up with something.

"Does he have a favorite band?" Jen, I was planning on calling her that until proven wrong, asked.

"I know he likes U2 and some alternative bands."

"You could get him concert tickets."

I nodded. "That's a good idea."

Chloe spoke up. "No good. U2 isn't touring."

Emma sat up. "Where's he from?"

"Vancouver."

She nodded. "When was the last time he went home?"

I shrugged. "It's been a while. Not since the draft. I know he misses his family."

She smiled and said nothing.

"What?"

Chloe smiled. "Take him home."

All of the women began chattering. Evidently this was a great idea.

I was confused. "How? It's the middle of the season."

Emma grinned at Chloe before turning to me. "They have four days between games."

"When?"

"Starting tomorrow."

"Oh, I know." Madi was practically jumping up and down. "You'll be at the airport when he gets back. You'll have both of your suitcases ready. You'll tell him to turn around and you'll go to the gate and fly to Canada!"

I looked around. No one was looking at her like she was insane.

"I can't pull that off," I protested. "Plus, he has practice. He can't just leave."

Madi held up her hand. "Let's see how he does tonight. If he's amazing. I'll text my dad and see if I can get him Sunday through Tuesday off. He'll be back for Wednesday's practice and the game on Thursday."

"You think that could work?"

She nodded.

Chloe piped up. "I went home with Reese around the holidays. It was only two days, but it made such a difference. It was like he recharged."

A few more women started nodding.

"Well, what are you waiting for Chloe? Let's find flights just in case."

She cheered and pulled out her phone.

"Come on, the game's about to start."

We moved as a herd to the living room where the TV was already showing the pregame. I found a spot between Emma and Sophia and tried to get myself to relax.

I was so nervous. This was a huge deal for Noah. It could determine the rest of his career. I knew that, but I really hoped he wasn't thinking about that. He needed to focus. Have his mind completely in the game. I'd been tempted to text him earlier, but I didn't want him thinking about anything but what he had to do the moment he stepped on the ice.

The announcers went on about the two teams and began to introduce the first lines. I cheered when Noah's picture came on the screen and they said he was one of the most promising rookies of the year.

Pride swelled in my heart. He deserved all the fame. One

day he would see that.

We all cheered when Hartman won the first puck drop. My eyes were glued to Noah standing a few feet in front of Olli as the puck came into the Fury's zone.

He was focused. I could tell he was in the right mind set. He wasn't letting anything get to him. I wanted to stand up. Pace. Anything. Sitting here in silence was too much.

"Come on ref, I know you saw that hooking!" Madi was screaming at the TV loud enough that the referee might have actually heard eight hundred miles away.

A few girls laughed, but the rest were agreeing.

Once Madi broke the ice, we all took turns standing and yelling. We might not be on the ice with the guys, but as I watched these women I knew they were the backbone of the team. They were just as passionate as their men.

The first period ended, and I finally relaxed. I took another sip of the apple cider and leaned back in the couch. The Fury were up by two and it didn't look like Denver had what it took to get caught up. They were much slower and looked exhausted already.

All of the grueling practices our guys went through were worth it. They made the team faster and stronger than their opponents.

By the middle of the second period, Madi declared it was time to text her dad. She said he wouldn't see his phone until after the game, but she thought if she caught him during the winning high he would say yes.

Chloe had found flights that would leave just thirty minutes after the team landed. It would be perfect, as long as Coach approved.

I should also talk to his parents. "Do you know how I can get ahold of his family?"

Chloe smiled. "Let me get their number."

I didn't question her ways. She had connections to everything, and just a few minutes later she texted me his parents' home number.

"Is it totally weird if I just call?"

Madi held up her hand. "Wait until we get the all clear from my dad first. Then go ahead." The women around her nodded. "It won't be weird. I'm sure he's told them about you. They'll be too excited to realize a stranger is inviting themselves to their house."

"Thanks." I laughed at her last statement. Hopefully they wouldn't notice I was inviting myself. I could always get a hotel. Yeah, I'd lead with that. I shouldn't assume Noah would want me to stay with them.

I watched the final period sitting with my legs bouncing. I had too much adrenaline in my body. I'd need to go for a run after this. No, if all went as planned I'd have to get home and pack our bags.

The final buzzer rang and we all jumped up and cheered. The boys had won!

We all hugged each other, and Emma even cried, but blamed it on the baby hormones, not the game.

We started to clean up, and I tried not to stare at Madi. She had her phone in her back pocket but wasn't checking it. Had she forgotten? Didn't she realize how important this was for me?

I threw away the trash and volunteered to take the bags outside to their can. I wanted a second to pull myself together. I returned feeling chilled and much less likely to tackle Madi to the ground to steal her phone.

Some of the women started leaving, telling me to let them know how it went. Soon it was just me, Chloe, Madi, Emma, and Sophia sitting in the living room. They were discussing more wedding things. I wanted to join in the excitement, but I couldn't focus. I just needed Coach to decide.

It was nearly eleven and I'd given up hope. I stood and started saying goodbye when Madi jumped up. "I have a text."

She stared at her phone and squealed! "You're good! Book the flights!"

Emma was cheering from the couch while I started jumping up and down with Chloe and Sophia. "I need to get my phone. I need to book them."

Chloe tossed it to me. "Already done."

"How?" We'd just barely been given the go ahead.

She shrugged. "I had a feeling and booked them during the second period."

"How did you pay for them?"

"I used some of my frequent flier points." She winked. "It's all taken care of."

I couldn't believe she would do that. "Chloe, I can't accept that. I'll pay you back."

She laughed and waved me off. "Between me and Reese we could fly around the world twice and still have miles left over. It's really not a big deal." She winked. "Plus, the Fury pays for the travel, we just get the points."

I shook my head, but she ignored me. Then I realized I needed to make sure it was okay to drop in on his family. "Crap! I can't call them this late."

Chloe shrugged. "It's good news to be woken up for."

"Just call them in the morning." I turned to see Emma standing. "Not much is going to change in the next eight hours."

She was right. I could wait. Then they wouldn't have to wait very long to see him. With my plan in place I finally felt excited. I couldn't wait to see Noah and tell him.

15

NOAH

I was exhausted. I couldn't wait to get home, crawl into bed, and be dead to the world for at least the next ten hours. The game had been amazing. Better than I could have expected, and the team gave me the MVP of the night. Any doubt I had about them accepting me vanished. We were all here to win, and we supported whatever decisions were made to get us the victory.

When the flight crew opened the door and we began exiting, I stood and started to stretch. I needed to get some energy for the short drive back to my apartment. I should have asked Colby to drop me off. Next time I'd remember how tired I am right now.

I followed the guys into the terminal and waved as we all went our separate directions. I rubbed my face and headed to the parking garage.

"Noah." I looked over my shoulder to Reese who was walking behind me. He pointed off to the left. I turned and saw Colby standing at the other side of the gate.

I looked her over for some sign of what was wrong. Why was she here? How did she get past security?

"Colby are you okay?"

She smiled at me uncertainly. A hint of excitement making her face glow. "Yeah. Everything's fine."

"Why are you here? What's going on?"

"Follow me." Without another word she turned and walked off in the direction of the public terminals. I wanted to ask more questions, but I had a feeling she would ignore them. What was she up to?

She led me through the airport and finally stopped in front of a gate. I looked around but couldn't see where it was going.

"Are you leaving?" I asked. "Did something happen?"

Was this how she was quitting? Bringing me here to see her off?

No, maybe it was her family. Was one of them sick?

The attendant at the counter next to us picked up the mic. "My name is Laura, and I'd like to welcome you all to flight three-forty-eight with services to Vancouver."

I blinked. Was she serious? She was going to Canada? Why had she brought me here?

Colby smiled and pulled something out of her pocket. She flashed a paper and I took it from her hands. A boarding pass. First class to Vancouver. With my name on it.

"What?"

She held up another boarding pass and my jaw nearly hit the floor.

"You're going home," she said.

"I am?" Relief washed over me. It was like I hadn't known how badly I needed to see my family until it was a possibility. I couldn't believe it was happening.

She nodded. "I'm coming with you."

I shook my head. There was no way. "I have practice."

"You have three days off. We'll be back for Wednesday's

practice and I promised Coach you'll work out while we're gone."

This was really happening? "Colby. This is amazing."

She beamed. "I'm so glad you're happy. I wanted to do something for you. I tried to get to the game last night but couldn't get tickets."

"So, we're going home?"

She nodded. "Is it okay that I'm coming? I don't have to."

For the first time since I saw her outside my gate, she looked doubtful.

"Of course. I can't believe you did all this. I can't wait for you to meet my family and see where I grew up."

I rubbed my face again. Sure, I was dead on my feet, but this was amazing. I hadn't been home in almost two years. This was a miracle. I knew she was doing this as a thank you for her birthday party, but this was on another level. If we kept going back and forth trying to top each other, we were going to go broke.

I knew that's not what she wanted or expected, but this meant so much to me. It was more than a birthday party thrown together in a few hours.

I wrapped my arm around her shoulder and pulled her in next to me. "Thank you."

We boarded the plane and settled in. I wasn't looking forward to another flight but going home was worth it.

"You were great last night." She was grinning.

I leaned back. "It was surreal. I can't believe I made that shot."

She grabbed my hand and I squeezed back. "This really means a lot to me, Colby. You already do so much for me. I know I wouldn't have survived this long without your help. You didn't have to do this."

She bit her lip, but I saw the smile threatening to peak through. I needed to thank her more often. "I wanted to."

I yawned and she released my hand.

"Take a nap. You look exhausted."

I waited to fight it. This was precious alone time I didn't want to waste, but my eyes were winning. I fell asleep before takeoff.

Colby woke me up after we landed. "We're here sleepyhead."

I blinked and looked out the window. We were already at the gate. I yawned and started to stand. The rows ahead of us were already exiting.

I followed her off the plane with just my small bag. All she was carrying was her purse. "Where are your bags?"

She waited for me to catch up to her in the terminal. "I checked our bags."

"You packed for me?"

"Of course. I couldn't let you wear a suit the whole time."

I looked down at my wrinkled shirt. Yeah, I didn't want to live in this for much longer.

"You really thought of everything." I felt guilty. She made my life too easy. I didn't even have to think anymore. She was always three steps ahead.

She smiled up at me. "Not everything. I didn't plan past us getting here. I didn't want to schedule too much in case there was anything you really wanted to do."

I appreciated that. There was plenty to see around the city, but all I really wanted to do was be home with my family. I'd have to show Colby around a little bit, though.

We walked down to the baggage claim. We were at our carousel when I heard voices shouting my name. I cringed and tried to stand behind Colby, like she could conceal me. I wasn't interested in getting mobbed today. I appreciated fans, but I just wanted to be normal today.

Colby stepped forward and waved. I looked up and realized it wasn't fans or even paparazzi. It was my family.

I hurried forward and wrapped my arms around my mom. Even though she only came up to my chest, she hugged me back fiercely. Her petite stature and strawberry blonde curls made her look delicate but raising three boys had made her strong. She could keep up with us and get us to shape up if needed. "Oh Noah. I'm so happy to see you."

"Me too, Mom."

I stepped back and took a good look at her. She hadn't aged much, same kind eyes and smile lines I'd known my whole life.

"Nice game last night, son." Dad stepped in, hugged me. "You look good."

"Thanks Dad." That was almost like giving himself a compliment. I got my blonde hair, height, and dimples from him.

My little brother, a miniature version of me, butted in and wrapped his arms around my waist in a grip I wasn't sure I could break. "Hey Evan."

He squeezed tighter in response. "I can't believe you won the game, Noah. That was crazy!"

He was fourteen and I knew from what my parents had told me that my being gone was hard on him. My older brother, Mikey, lived about thirty minutes from them, but was busy with his own family. Evan was left alone.

"Are we going to stand here all day, or can we go home?" Dad clapped me on the back.

Evan finally released me. "I want to show you the new hoop we got."

I laughed and nodded. "Sounds good. You might be the basketball star, but I bet I could still beat you."

Evan got a smug look. "You wish."

I turned around, realizing I'd left Colby alone. She was talking to my mom with our luggage next to her.

"Are you ready to head out?" Dad asked me and waved the ladies over. I took one bag while he took the other and walked out to the parking garage.

"I can't tell you how excited we've been since your call this morning, Colby," Dad told her.

I realized then that I hadn't questioned my family being here. How did they know we were coming and when to be here? I turned to Dad. "Colby called you guys?"

He chuckled. "Yeah, this morning. Introduced herself, but of course we knew who she was."

I'd told my family about her. She was my first friend in Salt Lake, but I hadn't mentioned the fake girlfriend thing. I'd have to clarify that.

"She told us she talked to your Coach about taking a few days off to see us and asked if that was okay. Your mom was screaming at that point. We've all been nerves and energy since then."

"Are Mikey and Brin coming over later?"

"Yeah, they'll be here for dinner."

I looked over my shoulder at Colby. She was a true wonder. Not only had she pulled this off without my knowing it, but she reached out to my family. That was pretty brave. Not that I should be all that surprised. She was used to reaching out to strangers to get them to do things for her all the time. I wondered how she introduced herself to my parents though. My personal assistant? My friend? My girlfriend?

I'd have to ask when she wasn't a few steps behind me.

147

The drive back to the house passed quickly with Evan and Mom quizzing us about the team, Salt Lake, and finally our relationship.

"It's just to keep the attention down, Mom."

Colby nodded. "Yeah, Bryce thought it would be a good idea. Keep Noah safe while he adjusted to the fame and glory of being in the NHL."

Mom smiled, but I could tell there was something she wasn't saying. "Well, as long as it's working for both of you, who are we to judge?"

"What's there to judge, Mom? Colby is my assistant and pretending to be my girlfriend in public. It's not that scandalous."

She nodded. "How many fake girlfriends plan a trip like this for the fake boyfriend?" She raised a brow and looked between us before turning around.

I looked to Colby to tell her to ignore Mom, but she was bright red. I didn't want to humiliate her anymore, so I let the topic drop. She had nothing to be embarrassed about. We might not be a real couple, but we were real friends.

They would understand once they spent more time around us.

Hopefully I could pull it off without Mom getting suspicious. If Madi and Chloe were already onto me about my true feelings, Mom would be on me in seconds. I needed to play it cool. The last thing I wanted was to make Colby feel uncomfortable. Not while she was stuck with me for the next few days. But I could use this time to get her to see me as more than her client.

We pulled up to the house and I was pleasantly surprised to see that very little had changed. Same meticulously manicured lawn and hedges. Same red door I'd helped paint in middle school. Same mailbox I'd hit when I was first leaning to dive. That was always a fear of mine. That things would change, and I would get left behind. I didn't want my family to get too used to me being gone. I wanted them to remember I was still their son and brother, even when I was in another country for months or years at a time.

"Is that the new hoop?" I asked Evan.

I pointed to the basketball hoop at the side of the driveway. It was nice looking, much better than the old rusted one Mikey and I played with when we were kids.

"Yeah, it's full regulation height so I can practice layups and free throws."

"That's awesome. You're pretty lucky. Mom and Dad never would have gotten that for me and Mikey."

Evan rolled his eyes. "That's because you both sucked. They bought you everything for hockey though."

He had a point. He might be the spoiled baby of the family, but my parents had supported my dream from the beginning. And look where I was now. I wondered if they knew back in the day I'd be one of the few who made it all the way. Probably not. No one thinks their kids will be one of the few, but they supported me anyway.

I'd have to tell them while I'm here how much it means to me.

"Come on in. I'll show you to your room, Colby." Mom was already walking away with her. Leaving us to deal with the bags. Mom was in heaven with another woman around. Growing up in an all-boys house had been hard on her. I thought she'd finally have that daughter she'd always wanted with Brin, but that hadn't happened like we all thought it would. Brin wasn't interested in getting her nails done or learning the secret to Mom's famous pie crust. She only cared about her job as an investment banker. She was glued to her phone and rarely joined in on family games.

With the way Mom was looking at Colby, I could see she was already getting excited.

I hated having to be the one to do it, but someone needed to burst that bubble of hope. Colby and I weren't really a couple. We didn't have a future.

Mom had Colby staying in Mikey's old room, she'd long ago turned it into a guest suite, but it would always be my brother's in my mind. I went into my room and sighed. Nothing here had changed either. My full-sized bed still had the same navy and white comforter I'd had in high school. My trophies and jerseys were hanging on the wall. There were even posters of bands I used to love covering one wall. I'm sure it drove Mom mad not being able to update things, but I loved it just the way it was.

There was a knock on my door and Mom stepped in. "We're having dinner in an hour, so rest up then come on down."

I nodded, expecting her to walk away. She hovered by the door and looked down the hall before stepping in. "I really like her, honey."

Here it was. "Mom, we're not really together."

She waved me off. "I know what I see, Noah. You two look at each other like you're in love. You might not realize it yet, but anyone can see."

"I'll be down in a bit." She picked up on the dismissal and left me alone. I didn't know how I was going to get that idea out of her mind, but it needed to happen. Colby and I were friends.

No matter what Mom, or even I, wanted.

16

COLBY

I was in love with the Malkins, and their home. I understood why Noah missed this so much. I couldn't imagine being away from them for a month, let alone years. They were everything my parents weren't. Everything I craved. Their home was lived in, not a show piece. I'd already walked the halls studying each family picture. His mother made sure I had everything I needed and was actually interested in getting to know me. She was the type of mother that would never, ever forget her child's birthday.

I freshened up and went downstairs where Evan and Mr. Malkin were sitting watching a show in the living room. A large Golden Retriever sat on the rug in front of them. His head popped up when I came down the stairs. His tail thumped on the carpet three time before he stood and came over to me.

"Hi there, love." I bent down and started rubbing behind his ears. He turned and leaned his body against me, getting comfortable as I massaged him.

"Oh Charlie. Leave her alone." Mary, she asked me to

call her that at the airport, walked out of the kitchen wearing a red apron.

"He's fine. I love dogs." It was a good thing too because Charlie didn't look ready to leave me anytime soon.

Mary humphed and walked back into the kitchen. It was open from where I was standing so I watched her move around, expertly stirring one pan and checking the oven at the same time.

"What can I help with?" I stepped slowly away from the dog to give him a chance to regain his balance on his own.

Mary looked around before pointing at a wooden cutting board. "There are veggies in the bottom drawer. Can you chop them up for a salad?"

"Of course." I was glad to have something to do. Mary was easy to get along with, but hanging out with brothers wasn't something I knew how to do.

"Thanks, dear." She turned back to the stove for a minute before moving to the counter with a hot pan. "So, tell me about yourself. Where are you from? Did you go to school? All the details."

I laughed as I took several bags out of the fridge and moved them to the counter.

"I'm from northern California. My parents and sister still live there."

"How old is your sister?"

"She's twenty-nine. She's married and lives pretty close to my parents. Well, for now."

Mary stopped and looked at me. "Is she moving?"

I shook my head. "No, my parents are selling their house and taking some time to travel."

Mary smiled. "How nice for them."

I nodded. It was nice. For them.

"Are you and your sister very close?"

I rinsed off a tomato and started cutting it. "We were growing up. I haven't been able to get home very much through school, so we've grown apart."

"Where did you go to school?"

"University of Utah."

She nodded. "Why there?"

Why indeed? "Honestly, they offered me a scholarship. I planned on transferring home after a year or two, but I fell in love with the mountains and the seasons."

Mary met my eyes and smiled. "Are you an outdoors person?"

"Not nearly as much as I should be. I don't ski or snowboard. I didn't have time as a student and now work is my life. I do like hiking in the summer."

"You and Noah. You need to find a good work-life balance."

I laughed. "We both chose the wrong careers for that."

"I suppose so. What made you decide to become a personal assistant?"

It was a common question I heard. Most people didn't understand why I'd want to work for someone else, basically managing their life. "My grandpa was really into sports. He passed that onto my dad who passed it onto me. I grew up going to football, baseball, basketball, and a few hockey games. I didn't have any athletic ability, at all, but I wanted to be in that world. My dad told me about assistants when I was in high school and I decided it was my calling. I love organizing and doing something different every day."

Some people didn't understand, but Mary smiled and nodded. "I can see how that would make life interesting."

"It has."

"Who knew it would lead to a relationship, huh?"

I laughed. "It's not real."

She pursed her lips and watched me. "You don't like Noah?"

I stopped cutting. "Of course, I do."

"You don't get along with him?"

"Yeah, I do. He's one of the most laid-back people I know. It would be impossible not to get along with him."

"And you're not attracted to him?"

I laughed, and I was sure my face was turning red. "Noah is very attractive."

"Then what's the problem? You don't have someone else you're interested in?"

I shook my head. Definitely no other prospects.

"Then why isn't it real?"

"Well, for now this is a part of my job responsibilities. It's just to keep people from taking advantage of him. We're trying to protect him and his career. Once the press dies down, we'll go back to being just athlete and assistant. Plus, I can't really date a client. It's in the contract."

Mary didn't look convinced, but let it go.

"Do you have any funny stories about Noah when he was little?"

She immediately brightened. "Oh, where to start."

"Hey. None of that."

I turned to see Noah walking into the kitchen and laughed. "Dang it."

"Thanks for the backup guys." He shouted to his brother and dad, but they ignored him. "I leave you two alone for a few minutes and that's where this goes?"

"Of course." I smiled at him and slid the lettuce off the board and into the bowl. Mary had two spoons sitting out for me, so I took them and tossed the salad.

"Good to know neither of you can be trusted."

I rolled my eyes and Mary patted his cheek. "I'll have the home videos out tonight."

"Don't you dare."

"You're outnumbered, Noah. Sorry." I shrugged and pretended to feel bad.

"Evan, Dad, you guys don't want to watch home video right?"

Evan's head popped up over the couch. "Yeah, it's been forever."

His dad started laughing. "Sounds good to me."

"You're both traitors. I'll remember this around Christmas."

His empty threat didn't seem to bother either of them.

There was a knock on the front door before it swung open. An older version of Noah walked in followed by a beautiful woman with jet black hair. She was wearing a crisp, white pantsuit and I felt seriously underdressed in leggings and a Fury shirt. I looked at Mary and Noah, but they were both casual.

"Noah." Mikey walked in and nearly plowed Noah over with a hug. Mary looked at them with a small smile. I could tell she was enjoying having all her family under one roof.

Noah broke away from his brother and turned to me. "Colby, this is Mikey."

Before Noah could continue, Mikey stepped toward me and wrapped me in a bear hug. "The woman who brought him home."

I laughed and waited to be set back on the ground.

"I like you already." His grin was so much like Noah's. It felt familiar.

"Thanks. I like you too." I looked at his wife to see if she would have a reaction to that, but she was still staring at her phone.

"This is Brin, Mikey's wife. Brin, this is Colby."

Brin looked up at me for a split second before returning her attention to her phone. "Pleasure."

Icy.

Mikey ignored his wife and turned the focus back on me. Unfortunately.

"So, you're the woman Noah has been talking nonstop about." I looked over his shoulder to where Noah was standing looking like he was ready to kill his brother.

"I don't know about that."

"Oh, I do. Every time I talk to him he goes off about Colby this, Colby that. You should have heard what Colby said today. Colby is the most incredible person to have ever existed."

"Alright, alright." Noah tried to pull Mikey away, but his brother didn't budge.

"Was that a secret, little brother? You didn't want me to tell your pretty pretend girlfriend you're a smidge obsessed with her?" His eyes stayed on me while he spoke to Noah.

My eyes darted between the two of them. I knew Mikey was just teasing him, trying to get a reaction. It was working. I'd never seen Noah look so annoyed.

I wanted to diffuse the situation. I knew Mikey was kidding, but Noah didn't seem to think so.

"Don't worry, Mikey. How about I tell you a secret to make it even?"

His features lit up and I motioned for him to come closer until I could whisper in his ear. "Can you keep a secret?" He nodded, enthusiastically. "Noah is the sweetest person I know. I think I'm a little obsessed with him too."

I leaned back, and Mikey looked at me like he didn't know if I was lying. I tried to keep my expression blank. I didn't want him to know I was telling the truth, even though

I was trying to play it off as a joke. If what Mikey had revealed was true, then maybe I wasn't alone in my feelings. The longer I was around Noah, the more I realized there was so much more to know. Each new detail made me like him more. I had a feeling seeing him around his family, in his comfort zone, would make all those feelings amplify.

I wasn't sure I was ready for that.

Luckily, Mary declared it was time for dinner and the moment passed.

I sat between Evan and Noah, across from Mikey and Brin, who still had her phone in her hand. Mikey kept shooting me looks to which I responded with narrow eyes. He better not open his mouth. I could always play it off, but part of me didn't want to have to.

The lasagna, rolls, and salad were amazing. I moaned after the perfect bite of cheese and noodle.

Noah smiled at me. "We need to get this recipe."

I nodded and looked to his mom. "Will you share it?"

She looked between the two of us and nodded slowly. "Sure."

"You cook?" His dad asked Noah, pulling my attention away from Mary.

"We both do." I answered as Noah said, "Yes."

We looked at each other and smiled.

"She does the shopping and meal planning and whoever gets back to my place first usually cooks."

"How domestic." Mikey said with a smirk.

I guess that didn't help with our argument that we were just friends. Pretending to be a couple. Did just friends cook together? Travel together?

Yes, they did. Of course. I was overthinking this.

Brin stood up. "We've got to go, Mike. My new client wants to meet."

Mikey looked at her like she was insane. "At eight on a Sunday?"

She returned his look with a vicious one of her own. "Yes."

He shook his head and stood up from the table. He took both of their plates and left the dining room.

Brin left without saying goodbye. Mikey came in and apologized before following his wife.

No one seemed surprised by their abrupt departure, but they didn't look happy about it. I would have to ask Noah about it later.

"Well, who's ready for some peach cobbler?" Mary's smile looked a bit forced. I felt bad for her, but she seemed to want us to move on.

"I'll help." I stood and collected plates before meeting her in the kitchen. "This was delicious, Mary. I can't remember the last time I ate this well."

If we stayed here too long I had a feeling I'd gain ten pounds.

"Thank you, honey. I know Noah likes to eat healthy during the season, but I couldn't resist making his favorite."

She moved to the oven and pulled out a dish with the dessert. She moved to the freezer and took out a tub of vanilla ice cream. "Can you grab five spoons?"

I did, then followed her out to the dining room. I thought she would have dished it out in the kitchen, but maybe bowls were already out there, and I missed them.

"We do this family style." She winked and set down the pan while her husband opened the ice cream and scooped some on top of the cobbler. Evan didn't wait. As soon as the ice cream hit, his spoon was ready, and he was in.

I laughed and watched as Noah joined in. Soon his parents were taking bites. This was a definite first for me, but I wasn't about to miss out. I grabbed a spoon and took some. It was incredible. The mix of hot and cold. It all melted on my tongue and I took another scoop.

Noah eyed me and tried to knock my spoon out of the way, but I elbowed him in the ribs so I could get my bite.

I smiled sweetly at him while he pretended to glare.

I looked up, remembering we had an audience and blushed when I saw all eyes on us. Everyone was smiling, even Evan.

"Sorry." I shrugged. "I fight dirty."

Mr. Malkin smiled at me. "Welcome to the family, Colby."

17

NOAH

"Are you ready, Colby?" I called from the hallway on my way downstairs. It was already nine in the morning and I wanted to get going if we were going to hit all the sites in time. I'd already finished a run and a weight lifting session at the gym with Dad. It had been a lot easier than my normal workouts, but hopefully I didn't fall too far behind. I'd just have to push hard on Wednesday.

"Coming."

I went down the stairs and waited for her in the kitchen. Mom had made cinnamon rolls earlier and they were waiting for us on the counter. Colby walked in and moaned.

"Those smell amazing," she said.

I handed her one on a napkin. "Another recipe we'll have to get."

Colby nodded while taking a bite. "Can't we just move here?"

I liked that she said we. A little too much. "Not yet, but maybe one day."

She smiled and took another bite. I couldn't believe I'd

said that out loud, and she didn't freak out. It was the first time I'd mentioned the future, and she just went with it.

What did that mean?

"Where are we going?" Colby asked after swallowing.

"I thought we could drive around the area. I'll show you some of my old stomping grounds, then we can head to Stanley Park."

"Sounds good." She took another roll before walking toward the front door. I grabbed a pair of keys, hoping my mom wouldn't mind us taking her car and followed her outside.

Mom and Dad were standing out on the sidewalk talking to a neighbor. I waved at Mr. Andrews and hoped I wouldn't get roped into a conversation about the weather. Again. We'd already had a twenty minute one this morning. . The older man waved back, and I blew out a breath. Free, this time.

Evan was nowhere to be seen. He probably was still asleep upstairs. Mom let him stay home from school, so we could hang out. That's why I wanted to get going, so we could be back in the early afternoon.

I opened the door of Mom's Subaru for Colby and she got into the passenger seat. I waved to my parents and got in without them stopping me. A good sign. We wouldn't be gone too long anyway.

"Are you ready?" I asked.

She buckled herself in and smiled. "Ready."

We spent an hour driving around. I showed her my elementary school, middle school, and the high school I'd technically graduated from, even though I'd spent most of those years in the major juniors in Seattle.

"This is where I learned to skate."

I pointed out the skating rink and she turned to look in

her seat as if the outside of the building would be interesting.

"This place is beautiful, Noah. I'm jealous you grew up here."

I smiled. I loved this place. "Hopefully, one day I'll live here again."

I watched her, waiting for a reaction. She nodded and looked out the window. I couldn't tell if that was a nod of agreement or approval. I wanted to ask but didn't have the nerve.

"Let's head to the park," I suggested.

It took us about forty minutes to get to the area I wanted to show her, and it was much colder than either of us were prepared for. My lungs burned with the icy air. We got out of the car to see the Lions Gate bridge and Siwash Rock before running back to the car.

She got in and laughed. "We're such babies. We live in the Rocky Mountains. We should be used to this."

I shivered and cranked up the heat.

"Sorry, it's usually so pretty out here. We'll have to come back when it's warmer."

She shivered and held her hands out in front of the vents. "Good idea. There's so much I want to see, but I'm not getting out of the car again."

I laughed and held onto her words. She wanted to come back. Did she see a future with me? As more than an assistant?

She entertained me the entire drive back to the house singing along to the radio. She wasn't a terrible singer, but she wasn't going to be making a career change either. The best part was her interpretive dancing and liberties she took with the lyrics.

She was dedicated. When she didn't know the words,

she made them up but sang them with such confidence that I second guessed a few of them.

I chuckled. "You do know the line is Saturday in the park, I think it was the Fourth of July, right?"

She smiled at me and continued singing. "Saturday, in the park, something 'bout the fourth of July."

I shook my head and listened to her serenade me.

This was the most laid back I'd ever seen her. She was carefree and full of energy. I didn't know what it was that made her this way, but I wanted it to happen more often. Was it because we were on vacation? Was she getting more comfortable with me?

When we turned onto my street, I saw Evan dribbling in the driveway. I parked on the street, so he wouldn't have to stop and got out.

"Hey, you up for a little one on one?"

His face lit up and I was grateful I'd made it back in time to hang out with him. "You're going down old man."

Colby stopped and Evan passed her the ball. She looked uncertain, but began dribbling. Taking careful steps toward the hoop. She looked up and winked at me before lifting her arms and shooting. The ball went in the net, without touching the rim.

"Did you see that?" Evan looked shocked, pointing at the hoop.

Colby just shrugged. "I've had basketball players as clients. One of them made sure I knew how to shoot. For situations like this."

She smiled and waved for the ball. I picked it up and passed it.

Evan and I met eyes before splitting to defend her. Colby turned and dribbled before turning again to the hoop. I stopped in front of her and put my arms up, attempting to intimidate her.

She laughed, filling the air with that beautiful sound. She twisted and took a step, but I was faster, wrapping my arms around her waist and pushing the ball away. I hugged her close while Evan stole the ball and scored.

"You're a cheater!" Her laughter rumbled against my chest and I decided holding onto her forever was a great idea.

"You're the cheater." I finally loosened my grip and she pushed out, still giggling.

"If you guys can't handle me I'm going to get something to drink." Colby waved and walked into the house like she lived here. I loved that she fit right in. I could tell my family loved her, and she seemed to like them. It was so unlike the relationship they had with Brin. I think we were all grateful for that.

Evan passed me the ball and I dribbled up the drive and tried to shoot, but he blocked me. I shook my head as he turned and scored. I couldn't believe my little brother could defend me. This wasn't supposed to happen. The natural order of things was me being able to beat him up and best him at everything.

Is this what Mikey felt like when I passed him up in the hockey league? I got invited to a senior level before him. He never acted upset, but it had to feel like this.

I didn't like it.

I stepped in front of him, blocking his path to the hoop. He tried to shoot but I swatted the ball out of the air. He was stunned for long enough to let me move around him and shoot. Ha! We were now tied.

This went on for a while. I lost track of time. I looked up, realizing the sun was lower in the sky and looked to the house. Mom and Colby were sitting on the porch with blankets wrapped around them. I'd forgotten the cold long ago. I'd removed my jacked and long sleeve shirt a while ago.

I looked to Evan who was sweating as much as I was.

"You good?"

He smiled. "I'm up, so yeah we can call it a game."

I let him have the win. He'd played hard and had bested me a few times. He'd gloat and hold this over my head for years to come, but it was worth it.

We headed inside, and I went directly to the bathroom to shower. By the time I was cleaned up and back downstairs, Mom and Colby were in the kitchen again.

"What are you guys making?" I asked.

They both looked up with smiles. "Your mom's showing me how to make her famous chocolate chip cookies."

I stopped and looked at the bowl. "No. Way."

Mom laughed. "Just because I wouldn't teach you doesn't mean I'm opposed to teaching someone...worthy."

My jaw hit the floor. She kept that recipe a secret. No one knew how she made them perfectly chewy, with the most perfect proportions of chocolate. Until Colby.

How had she managed to cozy up to Mom so fast? I was jealous, but also happy she was learning. That meant I'd have someone to teach me when we got back home. I'd have to convince her to reveal the secret, though.

"Your dad wanted to grill." Mom said. "Can you go get that started?"

I looked at Mom then out the window. It was cold, but I guess I couldn't complain after being out there all afternoon with Evan. "Sure."

I pulled on a coat and went outside to get it started. I waited for a few minutes before cleaning it off. When I went back inside Mom had a plate waiting for me, piled with steaks.

"I'll have the veggies ready in just a minute."

I nodded and turned to go back outside. I hurried to lay out the steaks, so I could get back inside. The sun was setting, and I didn't want to spend more time out there than I needed.

Mom was alone in the kitchen when I walked back in. "Where'd Colby go?"

She kept slicing asparagus and zucchini, not looking up, " I sent her to get cleaned up."

I laughed. "She's not a kid, Mom."

She looked up and smiled. "I'm well aware she's a beautiful young woman, Noah."

I ignored her and moved to the fringe for a drink.

"I like her," Mom announced.

I took a sip of water before turning around. Mom was looking, no, watching me.

"Me too, Mom."

"Then why aren't you doing anything about it?"

"I can't." I didn't want to discuss my feelings with her. Not while Colby could walk in at any moment.

"Don't be a fool, Noah."

"What's that supposed to mean?"

She put her hands on her hips. "Colby is an amazing person. She's beautiful, smart, incredibly sweet. She did all of this for you. I don't want you to miss out on something because you're afraid."

"What would I be afraid of?"

She sighed. "Settling down."

"I'm not afraid of that."

"You've been on the move since you were a kid. You've had an unusual life. You haven't had much stability because of hockey and I don't want that to carry on into your adult life. Hopefully, you'll be with the Fury for a while. I want you to be able to establish a life."

"I appreciate that, Mom. But it's not an issue. I don't have a fear of commitment or settling down."

"Then why aren't you and Colby together, for real?"

"One, we can't. It's a violation of our contracts." I shrugged. Plus, things between us were confusing. They didn't start out normal and we've gone completely out of order. "We've only known each other a few weeks. We went from having a professional relationship to fake dating. We haven't had time to consider that option."

"I don't want the opportunity to pass you by. She's been handed to you on a silver platter. I hope you realize that. If you were ever looking for a sign, I think her coming into your life the way she has is a pretty perfect one."

"I'll keep that in mind."

She narrowed her eyes for a moment before smiling. "You'd better."

"I think you just like her more."

Mom turned and didn't disagree. She slid the vegetables to me and I took the plate and walked outside to add them to the grill.

Colby walked back into the kitchen at the same time I did. She had changed into a pair of cotton joggers and a t-shirt. I was glad she felt comfortable here. I wanted her to feel at home. I wasn't sure why though. Did we really have a future?

As long as I didn't mess it up, maybe we could.

Seeing her here, in my world, made me want to try. When we got back to Salt Lake I was going to put in the effort. I'd take her out on dates, prove to her I was worthy. I wanted to make us work. If this trip proved anything, it was that we both cared about each other. We wanted to make each other happy. If that wasn't a great foundation for a relationship, I didn't know what was.

Colby smiled at me as she moved to the oven. She belonged right here. I didn't want this to be a one-time thing. I wanted to see her moving around my house, baking with my mom, talking to my brothers.

I wanted this to be our future.

The realization, probably spurred on by Mom, was a kick in the butt I needed to work my hardest to prove to the team I deserved a contract, so I could have a future with Colby.

18

COLBY

I thought things had changed between us. It felt like we'd made progress in Vancouver, like we'd grown closer.

Noah had hardly been around since we got back to Salt Lake. I ran into him once before his game. Just in passing. He was coming home from practice as I was leaving to run errands. He'd smiled, but that was it.

I didn't understand what changed.

Maybe his family had hated me. I thought we'd gotten along. I loved spending time with them, but maybe they didn't feel the same.

Or he realized I didn't belong in his world.

Maybe my feelings were completely one sided. The connection I thought we had could be all in my head.

Chloe invited me to sit with her at the game, but I didn't know if I was really in the mood. Cheering for him and the rest of the team sounded draining. I'd have to pretend I was okay in front of the Pride and that sounded exhausting, too.

At the check-out stand in the grocery store a magazine caught my eye. A small picture of me and Noah together was at the top corner. We'd made the national news? Granted it was a silly tabloid, but I was shocked they cared about a rookie hockey player. I grabbed a copy and read the tag line. "NHL's Favorite Rookie Returns Home: Is an Announcement Coming?"

Predictable and unoriginal.

I bought a copy.

I needed to go to the game. It didn't matter how I felt about it, it was my job to support Noah. Even when he was being grumpy.

He was already gone when I got back with the groceries, so I put everything away then changed.

He'd given me one of his jerseys to wear, so I put that on with a pair of ripped jeans. I made sure my hair and makeup was presentable before heading out. I sent Chloe a text to let her know I was on my way and to save me a seat.

Hopefully, Noah would be happy to see me in the audience. If he even noticed.

I need to find out what was going on. I couldn't live like this for much longer. It had only been two days and I was already wigging out.

"Hey Colby!" I waved to Emma and slid into the row below her. The normal suspects were there. I said hi as I passed to the seat next to Madeline and Chloe.

"Hey, there you are. I was starting to think you were going to stand us up." Madeline teased, but she had no idea how close to the truth she was.

"It's been a long few days." I hoped they wouldn't question me further, but that was wishful thinking.

Chloe leaned forward and was practically bouncing in her seat. "How was it? I've been dying to see you."

The women around us seemed to lean forward together. I smiled and spoke loudly enough for them to all hear.

"It was really fun. He showed me around where he grew up and we went to Stanley Park, which was beautiful. We mostly hung out with his family."

I looked around, hoping that would appease the masses. There were a few comments to which I smiled in response. I leaned back in my seat, again hoping that would be the end of it.

"If it was so great why does it look like someone kicked your puppy?" Chloe was eyeing me like she could see into my mind and knew I was holding back.

I didn't want this to turn into a group discussion, so I leaned toward her, so just she and Madi could hear.

"He's been off since we got back." I tried to whisper.

Chloe's eyes narrowed. "What do you mean?"

I looked out to where the Zambonis were prepping the ice. "He's been avoiding me. He's barely been home and hasn't said a word to me since we got home."

They both looked confused.

"But he was fine while you were there?" Madi asked.

I nodded and sighed. They didn't understand either.

"I wonder what happened." Chloe looked pensive, like she was trying to solve the mystery.

"I'm not sure. Everything was fine on the flight home. It was like the second we walked through the front door a switch was flipped."

Madi pursed her lips. "Maybe he's just been worried about this game. First time opening at home."

I wanted to believe that was it, but it didn't make sense. "He was nervous for the Denver game, but he talked to me about it. We've always been able to talk to each other, but now..."

I trailed off not knowing what else to say. I couldn't figure out what happened.

Chloe reached over and squeezed my wrist. "Just give him some time and space. He'll come to you when he's ready."

That wasn't the answer I wanted, but it was the best thing I could do right now. I nodded and sunk back into my seat. The game started, and I watched for Noah to enter. When he finally did, he was joined with Reese, Erik, Hartman, and Brassard. That was good. He was still on the first line.

If that wasn't the issue, what could it be?

I wondered that for the entire game. I cheered when everyone else did, but my head was miles away. I analyzed every detail of our trip and the flight home. Nothing had happened. Nothing I could pinpoint. I wanted to think if I'd done anything to upset him, he'd tell me. Maybe we weren't as close as I'd thought.

How long could he keep this up?

Maybe Madi was right. After a weekend off, maybe he was pushing himself to focus back on the game. Maybe he was stressed.

I'd know by tomorrow if that was the case. If he wasn't back to normal, then there was something else wrong.

The guys won, and I forced myself to smile and cheer with everyone else. The girls invited me to go down to the tunnel with them to wait for the guys, but I wanted to give Noah more space. I made myself available if he wanted to talk to me. I went to his apartment and took up residence on the couch. I worked through emails while watching a home renovation show.

The front door finally opened after eleven.

I sat up and watched Noah walk in. He dropped his bag to the ground and headed back to his room.

"Good job tonight."

He stopped and looked at me as if he was just realizing I was there. Had he not heard the TV? He met my eyes for the briefest glance and continued walking back. "Thanks."

That was it.

I'd waited up for him, and that was all I got? I wanted to follow him. Force him to tell me what was going on.

We weren't even this distant the first time we met. Now he was acting like I was a complete stranger.

I wanted to text the girls. I wanted them to tell me it would be alright. I wanted, maybe even needed, the assurance that things would go back to how they'd been. Our weekend had been so wonderful. What had changed?

It was no use staying up trying to figure it out, and I didn't want to bring the girls into this. If Noah was going through something, I didn't want to put more attention on him. If he needed space, the last thing he needed was more people watching him.

I went to the door and waited, the last shred of hope disappearing. He didn't come back.

I woke up to my alarm blaring at me. I quickly turned it off and laid back down. I reached for my phone and checked the screen.

I held my breath and... nothing.

Not a single message from him.

Fine. If he needed space I would give it to him. My worry was quickly turning into irritation. Two could play this game. If he wanted to avoid me that was fine. I'd make myself scarce. If he didn't want me around, I wasn't going to waste my time.

I checked my emails and wrote a to-do list for the day.

He had a few events coming up and needed his suit and tux dry cleaned. I considered even getting the ingredients for his mom's cookies, but frankly, he didn't deserve them. My other clients needed a few things done, so I finished their social media posts and planned out the rest of my day.

After I showered and got ready for the day, I hurried out. By the time I'd picked up his dry cleaning, emptied his PO Box of fan mail, and put in a custom order of dress shirts at his favorite store, my aggravation was boiling. I knew doing all of this was my job, but his silence was killing me. He usually texted me throughout the day, but day three of silence was getting to me.

My phone rang in my purse and I dug in to find it. I checked the screen and sighed. Still not him.

"Hey Chloe," I answered.

"Hi girl. You're missing practice."

I checked my watched and realized it was later into the afternoon than I thought. "I lost track of time."

"So, you're not avoiding him?"

I rolled my eyes. Of course, I was, but I wasn't going to admit that. "I just had a lot of things to get done today."

"Sure." I ignored her condescending tone. "You missed the announcement."

I stopped in front of my car and searched for my keys.

"What announcement?"

Whatever it was couldn't be public yet. I followed all of the team's social media accounts and had an alert set up for whenever the Fury was in the news.

"Howe's injury isn't recovering properly. He's done."

I found my keys and unlocked the door, so I could get in. "For the season?"

"No, permanently. He can't play again."

I froze with the key almost in the ignition. "That's horrible."

"It is. I'm going to miss him."

I couldn't say the same, since I'd never met him, but it was terrible anytime a professional athlete lost the ability to play their sport. It was life altering.

"So, what does that mean for the team?"

Chloe didn't answer for a few beats. "I talked to Madi, since she would know better. I had my guess, but she confirmed it."

"What is it?" I finally turned on my car while I waited.

"There's an open spot. Chances just got a whole lot better for Noah."

She confirmed what I was already thinking. This would be great. He'd probably relax a bit, maybe go back to normal.

"That's incredible."

"I know. As long as he keeps performing the way he has, he's set."

I sighed. Yeah, as long as he keeps it up. Which would require complete focus and dedication. The hope I'd just had about him getting back to normal disappeared. He'd have tunnel vision. No room to think or worry about me. I couldn't get mad at him for that either. This was his future. I couldn't get sensitive about it.

"Thanks for letting me know."

I hung up and headed back home.

Not home.

Noah's place.

Even though it had started to feel like it, that wasn't my home. I couldn't get too comfortable.

Now it was more important than ever to be supportive of him and make sure I was doing everything in my power to make his life easier. A contract was practically dangling in front of him. I couldn't be the thing that held him back.

Anything he needed, no matter how small, I would do. His focus needed to be on his performance.

This was my job. I needed to push my feeling to the back burner and start treating him like every other client.

19

NOAH

The moment Coach made the announcement about Howe, all eyes would be on me. I could feel it during practice. People were in the audience, more than just the normal Pride. I asked Erik who they were, and he said the names of different members of the board and even the general manager. I knew what that meant.

It was go time. I had to step up. There was a permanent spot open on the team. The potential for a contract was real. It had been a possibility before, but now, now it was a reality. The only thing standing between me and that contract were the people watching.

Colby wasn't there. I'd checked a hundred times throughout practice. I shouldn't have, but I couldn't resist.

This was the first practice she'd missed.

I pushed that out of my mind.

Coach yelled at me to meet him in his office after he ended practice. I went straight there, not bothering to stretch or shower before. Those things could wait. Whatever coach was going to tell me couldn't.

I sat across from his desk and waited. He came in behind

me less than two minutes later. He took his seat and looked at me.

"You've grown already, Noah."

I nodded. "This team has pushed me so much. I know it's only been a few weeks, but I feel like a different player."

"That's good. I can tell you've put in the work. You know what it takes to be in the NHL and you're willing to do what it takes. That's a great quality."

There was a but coming. I could feel it. Was this it? They were dropping me? Sending me back to the farm?

"With Howe leaving, we're going to need a defenseman to replace him. Permanently."

I nodded again. I'd already figured this out, but it was good to hear it come from him.

"I want that person to be you, Noah. You fit well with the team. You work hard. And you prove yourself at games. I always worry with rookies that they'll freeze when they get to the real games, but you never have. You're focused."

But? I waited.

"There's a lot at stake. I know I don't have to tell you that. You need to maintain the same level you have been. Maybe more."

"I can do that."

"I know you can, but I'm not the only one making the decision. I don't have the final say. You need to prove yourself to the rest of the office."

"I understand."

"Good. Now go stretch and ice. I'll see you tomorrow."

"Thanks, Coach."

I stood and walked back to the locker room. Nothing he said surprised me. I knew there would be pressure. I knew I would be watched. As much as I wanted him to pat me on the pack and tell me everything would be okay, and he believed in me, it didn't matter. I had to make sure the general manager, owner, and organization believed I had what it would take as well.

Erik and Reese were waiting for me when I walked in. Erik stepped forward first. "What did he say?"

I blew out a breath. "Just that with Howe being gone there's going to be an opening for a spot, and that I don't already have it. I'll need to work hard and prove myself."

Reese clapped me on the back. "Malkin, that's awesome man! You're the best choice. Anyone else would have to do what you've already done."

"What do you mean?"

"You've already proven your value to the team, and we all work well together. That's huge with the Fury. They don't take anyone, no matter how good someone is. They have to know the team will work together well."

I nodded, but I didn't really feel any better. Even though my dreams were a whole lot closer than they were yesterday, it felt like the opposite. Like I was farther away from obtaining my goal.

"Let's go out tonight. We'll all celebrate." Erik changed his shirt and waited for me to agree.

"There's nothing to celebrate yet."

Erik shook his head. "You're being too hard on yourself. As long as you keep playing like you have been, don't get in trouble, and don't piss anyone off, the spot is yours. That's worth celebrating."

I knew I wasn't going to win. He was just as stubborn as his sister.

"Fine. I just need an ice bath before I shower."

"Let's meet at Donovan's at eight."

I checked my watch. That gave me an hour to get ready. "Sounds good. Just text me the address."

I left them to sink into an ice bath. As much as it hurt in the moment, it was the only way I was able to endure these practices day after day.

By the time I was out and showered I felt a little more human.

I dressed and checked my phone. Both my brother and my dad had called me. They must have heard the news. I didn't want to call them back. They would all tell me that this was it. This was my shot into the NHL. I knew that. I knew this was a good thing. I didn't want to hear Mikey or Dad tell me I needed to focus. I didn't need someone else to tell me I had to work hard.

I'd been doing it my entire life. I'd never slacked off. I'd never done anything less than with one hundred percent effort. This wasn't going to be the time I stopped.

There was enough pressure on me without having to add their voices to the mix.

I was already doing everything I could to get that contract. I wanted it. More than anyone could possibly understand.

I wanted to be here. I wanted this team. I wanted the career. I wanted it all, so I could have a future with Colby.

I couldn't tell what was more important anymore. Hockey or her?

Both were huge aspects of my dreams for my future. I wanted them to go together, and a contract with the Fury was how I could get both.

I knew from the moment we landed back in Salt Lake that I needed to be serious. I couldn't slack off anymore. I had to throw myself completely into my training with laser focus.

I hadn't even been home much. If I wasn't at practice I was working out. I was with a trainer. I was recovering.

I hadn't been able to even talk to Colby since we got back, but I was doing this for her. For us. I needed to work as hard as I could now, so we had a future.

I put my phone into my back pocket and got in my car. I pulled up the address Erik sent me and headed there. I only wanted to stay for a few minutes. Just long enough for them to know I appreciated their support. I didn't have time to hang out for too long. I wanted to get home, so I could watch game film. We were playing Philadelphia next week, and they were a touch team. I wanted to study their plays as much as I could.

Donovan's was closer than I was expecting. I pulled up and found parking easily. I saw Erik's Lamborghini and knew I wasn't the first to arrive, so I headed in.

It was more of a bar than a restaurant, though it smelled like grease.

I walked to the back where I saw Erik, Hartman, Olli and a few other guys hanging out around a pool table.

"There he is!" Erik yelled when he saw me, and the guys cheered when I walked in and all I could do was shake my head.

"We already ordered some burgers, they should be out soon." Olli handed me a water cup.

"Thanks."

I got roped into a game of pool before the food came out. A few other guys filtered in, followed by some women I didn't recognize. They didn't seem to know anyone specifically, so I guessed they were the type that sniffed out athletes and followed them around.

I avoided them as best I could, sticking to the guys.

A waitress came in with a tray full of shots and a pitcher of beer. I eyed it warily. I avoided alcohol even during the off season. I knew most of the guys did too. I looked over to where the women had taken over a table and saw them smiling. They must have thought they were doing us a favor.

I continued my game against Andersen, a forward from the third line. I wasn't great at pool, but neither was he, so it ended up being a game of luck rather than skill.

"Next one who misses has to take a drink."

I looked up at him and laughed. "Yeah right."

His smile grew. "I'm serious."

"Neither of us drink."

He shrugged. "A shot won't hurt, too much. Just don't miss."

I rolled my eyes and took my shot. And missed.

He jumped up from his perch on the edge of the table and grabbed me a small glass. "For you, loser."

"No, man. I'm not drinking that." He could make fun of me or call me whatever he wanted. I wasn't going to do anything to mess up my mind or body. Not now.

"Come on, Malkin. Loosen up."

I looked around and no one seemed to notice the juvenile peer pressure that was taking place.

"Fine." I grabbed it and threw it over my shoulder instead of drinking.

"Nice try, bud. Now you have to drink two."

"I don't have to do anything."

He laughed and put his arm over my shoulder. You're way too uptight man. A little bit of this would take all that weight you're carrying around and throw it away."

I narrowed my eyes. It wouldn't solve anything. I might forget about my worries for a little while, but I needed a clear head. I needed to be at the top of my game.

"Come on. Just drink it."

I knew the nagging wouldn't end so I took the first shot and threw it back. It burned all the way down to my stomach. I was instantly reminded why I don't like drinking. It was gross, and it messed me up later.

"That's enough." I waved him off.

Andersen shrugged and drank the second one. I shook my head and walked away. I found an empty seat and Olli slid a burger my way. "You okay, man?"

I nodded. As soon as I got food in me, the alcohol would metabolize better, and I wouldn't feel as bad later.

I was a few bites in when he started talking. "I heard about what Coach said, but you're ready for this. I've seen what you can do, and you belong here."

I wiped my mouth. "Thanks man."

I wanted him to drop the subject. I came out to forget about it, but apparently that was all people wanted to talk about.

"You just got to keep your head straight and focus." Olli said before taking another bite.

"I will."

"I remember when I started with the Fury. I was only in the farms for a month. I wished I had more time to prepare, but it all worked out." He smirked.

I nodded again before standing. I appreciated what he was trying to do, but it wasn't what I wanted to hear right now.

"Thanks, Olli."

I stood and looked around. The women were all over a group of guys I didn't recognize. They sure moved on fast.

Erik and Reese were playing each other now, and Andersen was next to them. I wanted to avoid him, but he was blocking the way out.

Hartman walked up to me and leaned against the booth next to me. "How are you doing?"

I wanted to ask him to not talk about it. I was ready to lose it. "I'm fine."

He nodded. "Was it good to be home?"

I smiled, for the first time in what felt like forever. "Yeah, it was really great."

"Good. I'm glad you got to see your family."

"Me too," I said.

"That was pretty awesome Colby pulled that together."

"Yeah, she's pretty great."

He nodded. "Are you two really seeing each other?"

I looked at him, but he didn't meet my eyes. Why was he asking? Was he interested in her?

"No, it was my agent's idea. Hoping to take some heat off me."

"I know that. I'm just seeing if anything has changed." He looked at me out of the corner of his eyes. "She's an amazing girl. You're lucky. I hope you make sure she knows you appreciate her."

He walked away before I could process what he was trying to say. Was he interested in her? She was mine. He couldn't look at her. I didn't care how sweet she was or if he was my captain. Colby was mine.

I eyed Andersen and he smirked at me. He made his way around the table and picked up two more shots on his way. "You're looking a little wound up."

He offered me a drink, but I shook my head. "You really look like you need this. Don't worry about it. I'll get you a cab."

I eyed the clear liquid. I did need to relax. I was already feeling the slightest twinge of a buzz from the first shot. One more wouldn't hurt. I looked around to make sure no one was looking at me and took it. I eyed Andersen once before throwing it back.

"There you go."

Andersen started talking about a car he was looking at buying. He was into racing during the off season, and he found a new one he was interested in buying. I'd never been that into cars, but he made it interesting. Telling me how fast his cars were and how fast this new one was. That was all I understood. It didn't matter. He wasn't telling me about how I needed to focus. How I needed to be perfect. He didn't make me think about my family or Coach or how much pressure I was under. He didn't make me think he was into Colby. It was exactly what I needed.

Two drinks turned into four and I was feeling it. My tolerance was zero. I reached for a water. I needed to stay hydrated. The cup slipped out of my hand and clattered to the ground, spraying water and ice all over the floor. Erik and Hartman were in front of me.

Erik was holding me up.

"I can stand on my own." My voice came out slurred.

"No, actually you can't," Erik grunted.

Hartman was standing in front of Andersen. He looked fine. Why were they worrying about me?

The floor was spinning, just a little. "Guys."

Erik's voice drifted to me. "Come on, Noah. We're leaving."

We were walking. Then we were in his car.

"Do not throw up. I will kill you." Erik threated.

I nodded and closed my eyes, I didn't want to throw up. I wanted to sleep.

Something slapped my face and I pulled my eyelids apart. "No."

"Come on. I can't carry you, Malkin. You need to get up." He pulled on my arm until my body was out of his space-ship car.

"What floor are you?" He asked me.

I looked at the panel of numbers and picked six. I was pretty sure that's what I used.

He tugged me out of the elevator and into the hall. "Which way?"

I pointed, and he moved us. "What number?"

I stopped and stared at two doors. Why was it always so hard? "One of these?"

"You don't know?"

I shook my head.

I heard him swear but it sounded far away.

He pushed me against the wall and pulled out his phone. "Hi Colby. I know it's late. I'm sorry to wake you. What's Noah's apartment number? He doesn't remember which is his."

I pointed at one door and he watched me. I was pretty sure it was that one.

He shook his head and pulled my keys out of my back pocket. Dragging me to the next door.

"See I told you," I said.

Erik shook his head. "Come on."

He moved me in, then all the way down the hall to my room. When I saw my bed, I knew I finally found heaven. I could sleep. That's all I wanted.

I heard voices, but my eyes were stuck shut. I couldn't move anymore, just needed to sleep.

20

COLBY

I wanted to leave. I could have gone back to my place and let Noah deal with the consequences on his own. I wanted to. So bad.

But I couldn't do it. When Erik called, I'd come right over. It didn't matter that he'd been ignoring me. It didn't matter that I'd said two words to him in now four days.

He was my client. And my friend...I hoped.

I needed to be here, plus, he probably would call me for help when he woke up anyway, so I saved myself the trip back and forth.

When I woke up on the couch, I checked on him, but he was still snoring away. He didn't have to be to practice until eleven today, but he'd been going in so early I didn't know if there was something else he needed to be at.

I decided to wait until nine to wake him up.

Until then, I caught up on emails and tasks for my remaining clients. I showered and got ready, trying to make noise to see if it would wake him up on his own.

Nothing.

At ten 'til nine, I made coffee and grabbed some pain

killers and water before going to his room. I sat everything down on his nightstand before walking to the window. I pulled open the curtains and opened the blinds. It was the first time all week there had been sunlight in here.

He didn't move.

I went back to the bed and nudged his arm. He didn't stir.

"Noah." I reached down and shook him.

He mumbled but didn't wake.

"Noah." I shook his shoulders harder. "Wake up."

He groaned and rolled away from me.

"Oh no you don't. You need to wake up." I shook him until his eyes opened.

"Ugh."

"Wake up, Noah."

He threw his arm over his eyes. "Don't yell."

I rolled my eyes. "I'm not yelling."

"Why's it so bright?"

I moved away from the bed. "It's nine. You need to get up and get going."

He groaned again.

"There's coffee and painkillers on the table."

I walked out before he could moan and complain more. I had no sympathy for him. I couldn't imagine what he'd been thinking. Drinking during the season, with a game in just two days. He had so much on the line right now. Why would he do that?

I shook my head and went back to the kitchen.

I made myself a bagel and went to the TV to eat. I scanned the channels and stopped when I saw the Fury logo.

"With Howe gone, there's an opening to make Noah

Malkin a permanent fixture on the team. What do you think the odds are of that happening, Ron?"

The camera switched to the other anchor. "It's looking good, Hugh. Malkin has proven himself these past few games and if he keeps it up he might be looking at a rookie of the year title. As long as his star power last, he could be a great player for any team. The Fury have the best shot of signing him though. He seems to fit in well with the team."

"Can you please turn that off."

I turned to see Noah stumbling into the living room. He collapsed on the couch in just his boxers. I looked away before he caught me staring.

"Sure." I changed the channel but didn't pay attention to what was on. I was waiting for him to speak. To explain himself.

He remained silent, but I wasn't letting him off. Oh no. He was in trouble.

"That was quite the wakeup call last night." I broke the silence.

He cringed. "Sorry about that."

"What happened?" I tried to keep my voice calm, but I knew I sounded like a parent. Not that I cared at this point. If he wanted to act like a child, I'd treat him like one.

"I was just hanging out with the guys. One thing led to another and I had a few drinks."

I stared at him but his focus on was the TV screen.

"One thing led to another? You're a grown man, Noah. Things don't just happen to you. You made the decision to drink. You're not twenty-one, Noah. You could have been arrested. "

He didn't immediately respond.

"Why did you do it, Noah? You knew it was a mistake. You just got news that you could have a permanent position with the Fury. Why would you do anything to possibly ruin that?"

He slowly sat up and turned to me. "I'm aware, Colby. I don't need you to tell me that."

I shook my head. He was unbelievable. He was going to have an attitude with me now? After waking me up in the middle of the night?

"I'm worried about you, Noah."

He closed his eyes. "One night out is not something to be concerned over."

"It's not just that." He had to realize he was acting differently.

"What else then?" He opened his eyes and sat up. "What else have I done wrong?"

I narrowed my eyes at him. I barely recognized him with the way he was acting. This wasn't the Noah I knew. I didn't like this version.

"You've been avoiding me. You haven't spoken to me since we got back from Vancouver. Have I done something wrong? Are you upset with me?"

He stood up and faced me. "Not everything is about you, Colby. Have you ever considered that? I can have things going on that have nothing to do with you. You aren't the only facet in my life. I have other things going on. Things you don't know about. Things you could never understand."

I sat back. I hadn't expected that verbal beatdown. I didn't deserve it. I knew him. I knew this wasn't normal. There was something going on with him that I didn't know about, and apparently, he didn't want to share it.

Tears prickled my eyes and I blinked them away. As much as I cared about him, I didn't have to sit here and listen to this.

"Fine. I'm leaving." I stood to leave but he jumped up and blocked me.

"Look. I'm sorry, Colby. I shouldn't have yelled at you." He actually looked remorseful. It was the only reason I didn't shove him aside. "Things with the team... there's a lot going on. A lot of pressure."

I nodded. I knew it wasn't easy for him. He had a lot to prove to the coaches and the management. Just because he got called up from the farm didn't mean he was going to be offered a contract. They could decide to trade him, or send him back, without notice or reason.

"Noah, I'm sorry. I've been trying to do everything I could to make things easier for you."

He stopped me. "I know, and I really appreciate that."

"There's no reason for you to be treating me the way you have. It's not okay."

He dropped his head. "Dad said some things before we left." He sighed. "He's worried I'm getting distracted. I need to put all of myself into training right now. I need to be perfect during games. I need good press. I need to prove I can sell tickets. I need to show them that I'm worth being on the team."

"What does that have to do with being a jerk to me?" I asked, still not getting his mood change.

"I wasn't trying to be a jerk." He sighed. "I was just trying to clear my head. Refocus my energy on what's important right now."

"Am I distracting you?"

"No!"

I narrowed my eyes at him.

"Kind of."

I shook my head and moved away from him. "Noah, I've been doing everything I can think of to make this easier on you. I cook, clean, run your errands. I want you to succeed. What else can I do?"

He took a step toward me but I put my hands up and he stopped.

"I'm sorry, Colby. That's not what I meant. It's just... it's me."

I rolled my eyes. "It's not me, it's you? That's what you're going with?"

"Colby." He took a breath. "This is all coming out wrong. Dad just gave me a wake up call. He reminded me not to get distracted. Maybe I took things too far."

I shot him a scathing look.

"Okay. I definitely took it took it too far. I didn't mean to shut you out or be a jerk. This is the first time I've really had to balance hockey and a life." He paused. "I'm not doing a good job of it."

The fire that had been burning in me all day calmed to a simmer.

In a lot a ways Noah was childish. Immature. Inexperienced. But those were all results of his upbringing. He'd lived an incredibly sheltered life. He might be an adult, but he hasn't had the responsibilities.

He was also kind. Eager to learn and to be accepted. He was lost, but instead of being defensive he allowed people in. He wanted to get help. That was a strength most people didn't possess.

I nodded. "You're right. You haven't. I won't tolerate the way you've been acting. Even if it means backing out of our contract."

His eyes widened. "I'm sorry, Colby. I really am."

"Thank you. You have to promise me one more thing."

He nodded. "Anything."

"No more drinking?"

"Of course. I won't make that mistake again."

I watched him looking for any tells of lying. "Good. Now go get ready."

He left to get ready for practice. I fell back on my sofa and sigh. I'm glad things had been cleared up, but I was exhausted after a stressful night. My phone rang, and I answered without looking.

"This is Colby."

"This is Chloe." She mimicked me in the same voice.

"Oh hi. I didn't check the screen. I thought you might be a client."

"Do you need to go? You can call me back later."

"No, it's fine."

"Cool. So, how are you?"

I knew she wasn't really asking about me. Erik told her about last night.

"I'm fine."

"No puke to clean up?" She asked

I groaned. "No, thank heaven. I don't get paid that well."

She sighed. "I can't believe Noah did that. Does he know how much trouble he could have gotten in? He still can if coach finds out."

"I know. I'm hoping it all blows over."

"I'm glad you're okay." She paused. "Have you guys talked?"

"Yeah."

"Well? What's going on with him?"

I sighed. "I think it's just all the pressure. There's so much on him right now. From everyone. I think it just got to him."

"Yeah. I could see that." She said. "It wasn't smart, but at least he didn't get too drunk."

"Yeah, he just went to sleep and woke up with regrets."

"So, are things good between you guys now?"

"I'm not sure." I took a breath. "We talked, and I told him I would help with the load. He's worried about getting good press and exposure. He thinks it will help his chances of getting the contract."

"It definitely wouldn't hurt. All the press on Erik accelerated his career. The team loved it. If you can build up Noah's name, that will really help."

"What do you recommend, oh wise one?" I asked with a laugh.

"Well, I do have a bit of experience with this."

"It's your job."

She laughed. "You're right. How much time does Noah have for photoshoots or interviews?"

I pulled up his calendar. "Practice ends at four today, then a game tomorrow. He has an appointment and practice on Monday.

"Okay. I'll scheduled something for six tonight. I'll try to make it a phone interview, so he doesn't even have to leave the house."

"That would be great. I'll work on setting up a few interviews too."

"Good. You guys need to go out again. Make sure the paparazzi knows."

Ugh. I hated the idea of being those people who call and actually invite the vultures to follow you, but desperate times and all.

"Fine."

"Are they still outside the building?"

"They usually follow Noah if they see him but sometimes there are a few left."

"Go out and be seen. Make yourself recognizable."

"And do what?"

"I don't know. Get a coffee."

I groaned. "That's boring."

"It's pictures. Take out your phone and call me. Pretend you're talking to Noah and talk loud enough for them to hear you."

"No, that's too much." I'd feel too awkward.

"It's really not but do whatever you're comfortable with."

"Okay, I've got to get to work."

"I'll email you the details of the interview as soon as I have them."

"Thanks."

We hung up and I went back to my emails. I was shocked by how many people were interested in Noah. He was a star and he didn't even know it.

I searched his name and nearly screamed when images pulled up. Someone posted pictures of us in Vancouver. I clicked the link and found a full article about Noah taking me home to meet his family. There were pictures of us at Stanley park, Noah and Evan playing basketball, and me and Mary sitting on the porch watching.

It was creepy. I hadn't even noticed them there.

I took a breath and let it out. This was what we wanted. I sent the link to Chloe, so she could help spread it. This was the kind of positive press Noah needed, even if the article was exaggerating our relationship.

21

NOAH

Practice had an audience again. Instead of letting it get to my head I focused on pushing myself. There would always be people watching me. It didn't matter that they had control of my future. All I could do was prove my worth.

I was dripping with sweat only twenty minutes into practice. I still had a bit of a headache but ignored it.

"You doing okay?" Erik was sitting next to me on the bench.

"Yeah. Sorry about last night. I should know better than to give into peer pressure. "

He nodded. "I get it. There's a lot riding on your shoulders, but don't let the pressure get to you again."

"I won't." I wouldn't let it. Not again. I was stronger than that.

"Did Colby give you crap for it?"

I shook my head. "Not nearly what I deserved. She's actually helping me right now. Setting up interviews and stuff."

He grinned. "Working the press. Good idea. Sounds like something I would do."

"She'll probably get some help from Chloe."

He laughed. "Probably. Those two have gotten close."

"They have." I was glad Colby had found a group within the team. It would've been hard to ask her to come to practice and games if I'd known she was alone. The women in the Pride were as inclusive as the team. Another reason why I wanted to stay here. These guys were great, and I wanted to be a part of them.

"Back in boys." Coach Rust yelled at us and we threw our legs over the boards and joined our line on the ice.

Even though I was tired, mentally and physically, I didn't let myself slow down. I watched the puck like my life depended on it. I didn't let it get past me. Olli could have fallen asleep behind me. I wasn't letting anyone by.

Coach blew the whistle and we switched out again.

Hartman stopped by me and slapped my back. "Great work, Malkin."

I nodded and took a seat on the bench. Hartman was always supportive, but rarely gave out such blatant compliments. It was reassuring that I was doing the right thing. Hopefully, our observers noticed too.

Once practice ended, I stretched out quickly before resting in an ice bath. I sighed when I got in, actually enjoying the feeling on my muscles.

I lasted a few minutes longer than normal before showering and heading home. When I walked in, Colby was sitting at the table with her computer.

"Hey," I called.

She looked up and smiled. "Hi. How was practice? Sorry I didn't make it."

"It's fine, but it was really good."

"Good. Are you ready to get back to work?"

I eyed her. "What do you mean?"

"Chloe got you an interview with Sports Now Magazine, and I got you one right after with On the Ice. They're posting it on their website."

I nodded. I didn't really want to do these, but I knew I had to. "Where are they?"

Her smile grew. "That's the best part. They're both over the phone so you can do it from your bed if you want."

I laughed. "That's perfect. Thanks."

"The first one is in fifteen minutes. They sent me over their questions. Do you want to prep with me?"

She slid her computer toward me enough that I could see her screen. I read over the short list. "Nah. I got this."

"Okay great. Do you want me to stay for them?"

"Do you have somewhere to be?" I didn't mean to sound rude, but she was normally around for these.

"I ordered us dinner, so I was going to pick it up along with some promotional headshots the team wants signed before the game."

Of course, she was still working. The woman never stopped. "I've got this. Thanks for doing that."

"No problem." She stood up and grabbed her purse. "They'll call you. I have the questions for the second interview pulled up. They're set to call you at five thirty."

"Thanks."

She smiled once before heading out.

I read over the questions again. They were pretty basic. How was it playing in the NHL for the first time? What do I think of the team? What have been the biggest surprises? What do I think of the team's chance of a third championship?

I assumed they would ad lib a few questions as we went, but it wasn't anything I couldn't handle.

The phone rang and within a few seconds we were started. I tried to give interesting responses, but I felt like I was repeating myself from past interviews. I hated giving stock answers, but that's what happened when they all asked the same questions.

I finished without problems. Things had gone smoothly, and they said they would use images that they already had. I didn't bother asking. They were probably shots the team had sent them.

I closed out of that window and clicked around trying to find the next set of questions. I opened a document. Maybe she copied the questions onto it.

I scanned it and realized I was wrong.

This was her resume.

Updated to include her work with me. What was going on? Was she looking for a new job? A different client? Was she quitting?

She told me she noticed I'd been avoiding her. I hadn't meant to. I cared about her. So much. Enough to dedicate all of myself to training and performing the best I could. I wanted a future with her and to do that I needed to stay here.

I thought she understood. I thought we'd cleared things up.

Apparently not, since she was looking for more work.

I couldn't believe this. My phone rang, and I realized I had another interview. I minimized her resume and the questions showed. Perfect.

I answered and tried to push her out of my mind. I knew I wasn't as charismatic as I could have been, but at least it was over the phone. If it was in person, they would see how distracted I was.

The interview only lasted ten minutes, which was fine

with me. But that meant I was alone with my thoughts afterward.

What was I going to do? She was looking to leave?

I couldn't sit and wait for her to come home. I needed some space to think about things. I grabbed my duffle and headed back to the arena. More training was the only constructive thing I could think of.

I'd lift weights, maybe run. Push everything out of my head.

I expected the gym to be empty, but when I walked in Erik, Reese, and Olli were all there.

"Hey." Olli waved me over. It wasn't like I could avoid them.

"Hey guys."

"What's up? You look off." Erik said, and I was surprised he noticed.

"Nothing."

Reese laughed. "It's about Colby."

I looked up to see the three of them nodding. "Why would you say that?"

"It's always the girl."

Erik chuckled. "We all made stupid decisions, ended up looking like you, then fixed it."

Olli shook his head. "It's true. We should probably start having a dinner or something for guys when they start dating a new girl –."

"We're not really dating." I interjected.

He ignored my interruption. "It would save everyone a lot of time and pain. We just need to tell them they're going to screw up, go home and talk to her, grovel a bit, maybe buy her a gift, and all will be well."

"Says the married guy." I rolled my eyes. He and Emma

were perfect together. I doubted he knew anything I was going through.

"He's right, though." Reese looked at me. "I pushed Chloe away and had to fix things. So, did this moron. We've been where you are."

"I haven't done anything wrong."

Erik narrowed his eyes. "Haven't you though?"

I shook my head. "No. We were completely fine."

"Until?" He asked.

"Until I found her resume on her computer. It was updated to include working with me. She's trying to find another job. She's quitting."

Reese smirked. "Did you talk to her about it?"

"Obviously not, otherwise he would be with her enjoying dinner. Not brooding here with us." Erik said with a cocky look.

He was right, but I wasn't going to admit it.

Olli squeezed my shoulder. "You need time to cool off. Let's burn off some of that angst and you can leave with a more level head. Nothing good happens when you try to talk about something while you're still angry."

I nodded. "You're probably right."

"No, I definitely am."

I didn't want to admit it, but he was. There was nothing good that could come from me confronting her right now. The guys made it seem like there was a completely logical answer, and there probably was.

I'd jumped to conclusions, and I ran.

Colby didn't deserve that. She was doing everything she could to help me succeed. Why would she want to leave?

Maybe she just likes to always keep it up to date.

Maybe Bryce asked her for it.

There were plenty of possible explanations that had

nothing to do with her leaving. Why hadn't I seen that before? Why did I storm off? Why did I assume the worst?

It was because I cared. I was scared of losing her. I couldn't handle it.

Things had changed between us, especially in Vancouver. I didn't want to go back to being just friends. I wanted her.

I wouldn't screw this up.

Erik spotted me while I did bench presses, then we switched.

"How did you tell Madeline how you felt about her?"

I expected him to laugh or maybe tease me, but he blew out a breath as he lifted the weight then stopped. He turned on the bench until he was facing me.

"I screwed up. I pushed her away." He shook his head. "I thought I lost her. I thought she was getting back together with her ex. It was a humbling experience. I had to lay everything out for her. She could have walked. She had every reason to, but she stayed. She told me she felt the same and the rest is history."

I nodded. "Think that's what I'm going to need to do."

He smirked. "It's worth it."

22

COLBY

I listened to Chloe's advice and made sure I was seen as I left. I walked through the front doors of the building and down the street to the restaurant I'd ordered from. A few photographers followed me. I couldn't believe they thought I was interesting enough to be filmed walking down the street. On the way, I called and asked the printer to deliver the photos, to which they thankfully agreed.

I got our food and walked back making sure to smile.

"Is Noah ready for tomorrow's game?" A paparazzi called out.

I looked over my shoulder and grinned. "Yes, he's been working so hard and really pushing himself. He's ready."

"Are you guys getting serious?" This was a different voice. "Will you be the third couple to get engaged?"

I tried not to blush and forced my smile not to waver. "I don't know about that. We're enjoying this stage right now."

That was a good answer, right? I was great at prepping other people for interviews, but me? Not so much. I was a behind the scenes kind of girl.

"Do you think he has what it takes to stay on the Fury?"

I turned in the direction of the voice, unsure which person asked. "Of course. I've never known an athlete more deserving of where he is."

They continued shouting questions, asking me to turn or pose, but I waved and walked into the building.

That was exhausting. Chloe must be used to it from her position with the team. Plus, Erik was one of the more popular players with the media. She was probably used to fielding these questions.

I finally relaxed when I got to the door and unlocked it. I stepped inside and instantly noticed how quiet it was.

"Noah?"

No response. I set our food on the counter and went to the table where my computer was sitting.

I woke it up and my resume was up on the screen.

"Oh no."

I'd completely forgotten I left it up. He had to have seen it while looking at the questions. I'd been working on updating it since my contract with my other two clients would be up at the end of the month.

My contract with Bryce for Noah was great. I wouldn't have to worry about finding more clients, but I didn't want to risk depending on him. What if he didn't get the contract? What if he got picked up by another team? What if he got sick of me?

There were endless possibilities and I didn't like being vulnerable. I knew most people only had one job. Most PA's only worked for one person, but I didn't like that. I wanted to always be busy and always be secure.

I dug my phone out of my purse and called him. It rang but went to voicemail.

Great.

I had no idea where he was or what he was doing. Hopefully it wasn't a repeat of last night.

Crap. Now that's what I would worry about.

I debated calling some of the guys, but I didn't want to worry them, or have them thinking I'm crazy.

No, he would come back. I'd just have to wait.

I put our food in the fridge and went to the couch. I could wait him out.

I turned on the TV and found a makeover show to entertain myself.

Two episodes later he still wasn't back. Not only was I worried, but I was hungry. I called him again, but he didn't answer.

It was like déjà vu.

Well, if he wants to disappear on me, I'm not waiting for him to eat.

I went to the kitchen and heated up my enchiladas. He was on his own. Once my food was ready I got a glass of water and went back to the couch to eat. I was almost done when I heard a key in the door.

It swung open and Noah walked in, a sweaty mess. "Hey."

I stared at him. That was it? He disappears and ignores my calls and all I get is a 'hey'? Like everything was normal.

"Where did you go?"

He tossed his bag to the ground and finally looked at me. "I needed to clear my head."

I wanted to ask about the resume but didn't want to flatter myself. He wouldn't have gotten that upset about it.

"Were the interviews bad?"

He shook his head. "They were fine."

"Then why did you leave?"

He sighed and rubbed his face with both hands. "I saw

your resume on your computer. I wasn't trying to snoop. I was looking for the questions for the second interview and found it. It freaked me out." He paused before looking me in the eyes. "Are you quitting?"

I felt guilty that was his first thought. "No."

"Then what are you doing?"

I set my plate on the coffee table. "My contracts with my two others clients are done this month and I wanted to make sure I had more work."

He met my eyes and stared. "Are you sure that's it?"

I nodded. "I'm not going anywhere, Noah. Not as long as you want me here."

He sighed and collapsed on the couch next to me. "They were right."

"Who?"

"The guys. I went to work out. Erik, Reese, and Olli were already there. They told me I was crazy. That I just needed to talk to you."

I smiled at him even though he was staring at the ceiling. "They're pretty smart."

"They learned through experience."

I laughed. I could only image what the girls had put them through.

He turned and met my eyes. "You're not leaving?"

I shook my head. "Nope."

"Promise?"

"Yes."

"Good."

He looked so relieved I couldn't help but laugh. "You really think it would be that bad without me? I'm sure Bryce would find someone within a few hours to step in."

He blinked. "They wouldn't be you."

He sounded so sincere, vulnerable.

"You would miss me?"

He nodded. "It would destroy me."

I sucked in a breath. "Because I do so much for you?"

He shook his head. "Because you're the first thing I think about when I wake up, and the last thing I think about when I fall asleep. You've become a part of me. When I get good news, you're the first person I want to tell. When I'm frustrated or nervous, you always know exactly what to say to help me. You get me. You know me better than anyone else. I can't imagine life without you."

I couldn't believe what I was hearing. He was saying everything I wanted to hear, but something was missing. He could mean I was his best friend. It didn't mean he had the same feelings I did.

I smiled. "Noah, I could say all those things about you."

"Because I'm you're client?"

I shook my head.

We stared at each other. Neither willing to take the leap.

"Will you be my date to the dinner after the game?"

I almost laughed at the change of topic. There was a fancy pants dinner for the team and season ticket holders and a few more important people. I'd picked up his tux for it. I thought if he wanted me to go with him he would have asked a while ago.

"You expect me to find a black-tie event worthy dress in a day?"

He smiled. "I believe in you."

I rolled my eyes. "Sure, all you have to do is put on the tux in your closet. It seems so easy."

"Chloe will help you."

He was right. I'd have to let her know now and maybe she could help me out.

"Okay."

"You'll come with me?"

I nodded.

"As my girlfriend?"

"Of course, isn't that what we are?" We'd been a couple for weeks. I didn't understand why he needed to ask.

He didn't respond immediately, but finally nodded. "Yeah."

"Okay, good. Get your food. It's in the fridge. I have work to do." I stood and grabbed my laptop. I needed to start searching for places in the city that would have an appropriate dress and see how soon I could get in.

I looked up when Noah sat back down next to me. He smiled at me then reached for the remote and changed it to a game. Of course.

23

NOAH

This was going to be a long day. When I got up Colby had left me a message saying she was going to be running errands all day but would be at the game. I appreciated the thought of letting me know where she was. I probably should have done that last night.

I showered and dressed in my suit before leaving for the arena. The game was early, at five today, so I needed to get down there. We had press meetings before, so we would have time to get ready for the dinner tonight. From what the guys had told me, this was a pretty big night.

Chloe was in charge of it and it was mostly to give people the opportunity to meet and mingle with the players. She had them every few months, inviting the season ticket holders, and sponsors. She said when people felt like they knew us on a personal level they were more likely to spend money. That was fine by me. Anything I could do to help the team was something I was on board with.

"Malkin, you're at the first table with Erik and Reese." I nodded to the assistant with the headphones directing us. I handed off my bag and went to the table. There were three mics set up, so I sat on the left and waited for the other guys.

A few reporters and photographers were already in place, waiting.

I smiled and nodded at a few who made eye contact. I wasn't used to being here early. I was usually shuffled in somewhere in the middle and immediately thrown to the wolves.

"How's it going, Malkin?"

I smiled at the man sitting in the front row.

"Great. I'm excited for the game."

"You're still starting?"

"Yes, sir."

He nodded but didn't ask anything else. That was fine with me.

A moment later, Erik and Reese walked up and joined me. Reese leaned over and clapped my shoulder. "How you doing?"

"Good."

Erik smirked at me. "Did you talk to her?"

I looked around, making sure no one was paying attention to us. Most of the reporters were on their phones and the guys with cameras were looking at their equipment.

"Yeah, we're good. I asked her to come to the dinner tonight with me."

Reese started laughing and Erik shook his head.

"What?"

Reese looked at me with pity. "You just now asked her? You've known about it since you got here."

I shrugged. "It wasn't really on my radar. I didn't realize it was like prom."

Erik smirked. "It's worse. This matters more."

Reese nodded. "There are way more eyes on this. I hope she can find a dress in time."

Guilt suddenly filled my belly. I didn't think it was that big of a deal. I figured she had something she could wear.

"Will Chloe have something she can borrow?"

Reese shrugged. "Not that she hasn't already been photographed in. If Colby shows up in one, people will talk about it."

Geez. I had no idea it was this cut throat. I thought it was just a fancy dinner. I didn't realize there was a fashion show involved.

"She left early this morning to try to find one."

"Poor Colby. Chloe can't even help her. She's completely booked all day setting up. I'd be surprised if she can make it to the game."

I cringed. Colby was probably panicking.

Erik pulled out his phone. "I'll text Madi and have her help her. Hopefully her day isn't too packed, and she can get someone else to cover her patients."

"That would be great. Thanks."

I should probably be helping too but I didn't know what I could do.

Someone walked on stage and introduced us, as if the reporters didn't know who was sitting in front of them. They went through ten minutes with this group before moving to the next table.

It all passed in a blur. I did my best to answer when questions were directed at me, but I was worried about Colby. It wasn't fair that I did this to her. I hated that I made her stress. As if she didn't have enough going on in her life.

When we had a break, I texted her to see how she was doing, but I didn't hear back before I had to head into the team meeting.

Coach had us pumped. I already felt good about playing Michigan, but after the talk I knew we had this in the bag. As long as I played like I had in practice, we would be fine. I needed to focus on my only job. Block the puck. I wasn't letting it past me. I wanted Olli to be able to take a nap.

We finally were free to go to the locker room and hang out before changing. A few of the guys started a game of foosball. Others were snacking and chatting, but I needed to block everything out.

I found a recliner, put on headphones, and zoned out.

My phone vibrated, and I contemplated ignoring it, but if it was Colby I wanted to know. I checked, and she had sent me a text. I opened my phone and she said she was set and on her way to the game.

I laughed and closed my eyes. She did it. I knew if anyone could pull it off it would be her. She was an expert in dealing with time constraints and impossible tasks. She could add that to her resume. I'd back her up.

I focused on the music. Visualizing plays.

There was a tap on my shoulder and I opened my eyes to see Hartman standing over me. I pulled off my headphones. "Yeah?"

"It's time. Go change out."

I turned off my music and went to my locker. This was when my body went into autopilot. It was all muscle memory that got me dressed and out to the ice to warm up. I did a few laps to warm up my legs and looked into the section where the Pride sat. Colby was sitting with Madi and Emma in the second row. She smiled and waved, and I nodded as I passed.

She made it. She was here to see how hard I've been working this week. I knew there were people watching who had more of an influence on my life. The owner, coaches, and general manager to name a few. I was playing for her tonight. I wanted to show her I was working as hard as I could to keep us together.

She might not have understood that until I explained it to her, and that was my fault. This whole relationship and communication thing was new to me.

I was ready. I just wanted the clock to start. I went through the motions of them introducing our team and skating out with the guys. I barely stood still long enough for the national anthem. When Hartman went to the center for the first puck drop I was struggling to contain my energy.

I shook my head.

It was time to focus. The second the puck hit the ice, Hartman passed it to Erik. I watched it like a hawk stalking its prey. I wasn't going to let the puck get past me.

Michigan got the possession and turned toward me. I watched their center come down the ice and took my chance. When he went to pass it, I was there. I hit it behind him and straight to Reese. He charged toward their goal and took a shot.

It went in. The noise in the arena was near deafening.

I nodded when Reese looked back at me.

I was in the zone. This game mattered. I could feel it. This would be the one that decided my fate.

I wasn't going to give them any reason to pass on me. I would not slip up.

When our line changed I hurried to the bench and took a few gulps of water. As much as I wanted to rest, I wanted to be out there more.

"Nice job, Malkin." I gave a half smile to Hartman before turning back to the game. A few other guys agreed, but my attention was on the ice.

My leg was bouncing. I wanted to get back out there.

The puck passed by our left wing and into our zone. I held my breath while the defenders tried to block, but the Michigan center was able to shoot. I almost closed my eyes, but I had to watch. Olli caught it with his glove, inches from going in.

I sighed and Coach yelled at us to get ready. I was. A whistle blew, and our line went back on.

We ended the game with three goals to zero. I couldn't take all the credit, but I felt like I'd done my part. I was proud. That was all I could ask for.

A few guys slapped me on the back on our way through the tunnel. They knew how hard I'd worked, and I appreciated that. My job wasn't over though. I wouldn't lose this intensity. I couldn't relax until I had a signed contract. Maybe then I could breathe again.

"Hurry up guys, we need to get to the Capitol building in thirty minutes." Hartman usually gave a short speech after the game, but not tonight. We might have won, but we were far from being done for the day.

My tux was waiting for me. I'd completely forgotten about it. Colby must have brought it for me. She was incredible. And intuitive. It was like she knew what I needed before I did.

I smiled and hurried to shower. Luckily, there wasn't much I had to do to get ready. Get dressed and comb my hair. Done.

I waved to the guys as I headed out. I pulled out my phone and called Colby.

"Hey." She answered.

"Hi, where are we meeting?"

"I drove over with Madi, and we just finished changing. I'll meet you in the parking garage."

"Sounds good."

I went to the elevator and rode up. There were a few people milling around. I waved to my teammates. It was strange seeing them so cleaned up. We had to wear suits to games, but tuxes were next level. I couldn't help but laugh at the few with long, full beards. They seemed out of place with a black bow tie.

"There you are."

I turned and saw Colby walking toward me. She was wearing an elegant silver gown. Lace covered her arms and shoulders, but the material changed to a light, shimmery silver at her waist. She looked like a princess.

I smiled. "Hello, Cinderella." She looked stunning.

She smiled and touched her hair. It was pulled up in fancy bun. "You look quite dapper."

"Thanks. I don't think I look worthy of being next to you, though."

She blushed. "You think I look okay?"

I stepped forward and put my hands on her shoulders. "You're breathtaking."

She looked up at me through her thick lashes. "Thank you."

"Are you ready?"

She nodded once.

I bent down and kissed her forehead. I couldn't resist, and when she didn't stop me I added a kiss to her cheek, for good luck.

I led her to my car and made sure her dress was all in before shutting her door.

There was an actual red carpet set up in front of the entrance to the building. I looked over at Colby and saw her staring, like a deer in headlights.

"We got this." I tried to reassure her.

She looked at me and smiled. "Okay."

The valet opened her door and I stepped out to meet her. Cameras were flashing faster than I knew was possible. I took her hand and led her up the stairs. When we got to the top there were people waiting to direct us. They had us take pictures together down the carpet and asked for just me as well.

"I think we're almost done." I whispered next to her head as we smiled. She was doing well, but I was over this. I knew it was a part of being a professional athlete but that didn't mean I liked it.

"You're all set. Head on in."

I thanked our assistant and took Colby's hand. She sighed and seemed to relax with each step we took away from the cameras.

"You ready to have some fun?" I whispered.

She laughed. "How do you know this will be fun?"

"Cause Chloe planned it?"

"Good point."

There were already plenty of people walking around and sitting at the tables. Chloe greeted us and pushed us to the dance floor.

"There's supposed to be dancing before dinner and no one is. Go start."

I looked to Colby, and she didn't seem eager to argue. "May I have this dance?"

I led her in the direction of the dance floor and turned to her when we were in the center.

She put her hands on my shoulders and finally smiled. "This is when you put your hands on my waist."

I followed her direction and then froze. "Now what?"

Her eyes narrowed. "You've never danced?"

I shook my head. "Prom was not a priority when the championships were at stake."

She laughed and began taking steps to one side then the other. "Just sway."

I followed her and felt a little ridiculous. Not only were we the only people dancing, but everyone watching could see how clueless I was.

"Relax." She smiled up at me and I decided to ignore everything else.

Just focus on her. I met her eyes and smiled. "Thanks for coming tonight."

"I wouldn't miss it."

"I'm sorry I didn't ask sooner. I really didn't realize it would be such a big deal." I dipped my head. "This is my first dance."

"You missed prom?"

"We had a game." I shrugged. "It wasn't a big deal at the time, but now I felt like I missed out on a life experience."

She laughed. "Well, next time you need to give me more notice."

"I promise." I leaned forward and kissed the top of her head. "But you pulled it off. You looked amazing."

Her blush returned. "Thanks, Noah."

She looked away and I studied her. She was gorgeous. She was kind and caring. She was my best friend. But what I felt for her was beyond that. Mom was right. The perfect girl had been handed to me on a silver platter and so far, I'd been an idiot.

I didn't want to keep making that mistake.

"Colby?"

She looked back at me.

"I need to tell you something." I finally got the words out.

"Okay." She looked a little worried. I guess I wasn't starting this off the best way I could have.

"We've only known each other for a few weeks." She nodded. "But I want you to know, you're so much more to me than my assistant or even my friend."

She stopped dancing for a moment before starting again.

"Everything I told you last night is true. You're all I can think about. I'm working as hard as I can to get that contract, so I can stay here. Stay with you." I smiled. "I want to be with you."

She blinked, and her mouth opened, just barely.

"Colby, I know this might be moving too fast. I know we did things out of order, but I want to be with you. I want us to be a couple, for real."

She looked shocked. "Really?"

I nodded.

"Noah. That's what I want. I want to be with you."

"What about the contract? What will Bryce do?"

She shrugged. "We'll figure it out."

It felt like my heart had shot through the ceiling and was flying somewhere near the moon.

I bent down and kissed her. I didn't care if anyone was looking. She pressed into me and deepened the kiss. A moan escaped me, and I tried to pull back before I embarrassed myself, but her hands found their way in to my hair and pulled me closer.

It was heaven. Being with her. Having her know how I felt. It was all perfect.

"I'm falling for you." I kissed her again before she could respond.

24

COLBY

L ast night had been a dream. The day was a bit of a nightmare, but in the end, it was worth it. Madi had been a lifesaver. She knew the store that would have exactly what I needed.

Seeing Noah in a tux had almost been too much. He was so handsome. I didn't want to share him with the rest of the world, but I knew it was what we had to do.

The dinner and rest of the night had been a blur, every moment after Noah confessing his feelings seemed to melt together.

I reached for my phone and saw dozens of messages and notifications. What was going on?

I clicked on the first one. It was a link to Sports Now's website. Did they already have his interview posted?

I read the headline and my heart froze.

"Rookie falling for his princess"

Seriously?

I scanned the article. There were pictures of us walking the red carpet, then a picture of us dancing together. Our heads were bent together, smiling.

Someone told the press what Noah said? They didn't hear the first part of our discussion, thankfully, otherwise they would have known we weren't really together. They'd heard him say he was falling for me.

That was a private moment.

It was just for me and him.

How did this get out?

Press wasn't allowed inside. Chloe was strict about that. So how did they get this picture and quote?

I looked through my texts. There was one from Bryce. I hoped he wasn't upset about it.

I clicked on his name and read. "Good job!"

What? What was that supposed to mean? I responded asking him. I wasn't going to play the guessing game.

He replied quickly. "The press ate up the story. Noah's everywhere."

He thought I fed this to the media? Of course, I didn't. But someone did.

Who would do that?

Who would sell him out?

Tears burned my eyes, but I pushed them away. I felt violated. Exposed.

That was such a precious moment to me. Who would do this?

Noah was the only other one in the area. He was the only one who knew. But he wouldn't.

Would he?

He was doing everything he could to get the contract. That didn't mean he would do this.

I had just told him good press was crucial.

He wouldn't.

But he was the only option.

I couldn't believe that.

I got out of bed and threw on some sweats and a coat. I needed to leave. I needed out.

I grabbed my keys and went down the elevator. I was too upset to drive, so I went out the front doors and was immediately swarmed by cameras.

"Are you engaged?" A voice shouted, and I ignored it.

"Are you the lucky number three?"

How had they found me? They were never at my building before.

"How did he ask?"

"Are you pregnant?"

That one really bugged me, but I pushed through them and hurried to the closest café. They didn't follow me in while I ordered my coffee.

I wanted to hide inside, but people were staring at me. They knew I was the reason for the commotion and I didn't want to disrupt anyone else. Just because I'd willingly brought this on myself didn't mean I needed to bother anyone else.

I walked out and ignored their comments. I should've brought headphones.

I didn't want to listen to them. I didn't want to hear what they were saying. I also didn't want to go home.

I was stuck. Neither option was appealing.

I crossed the street and walked into the park. If I answered them would the questions stop, or would that just encourage them to ask more?

Probably the latter.

They were like a wild animal, rabid for information.

I wandered until I ended up at the pond. I looked at the bench. The one we'd sat on during our first official outing as a couple. It almost seemed fitting. I walked over and took a seat.

I sipped my coffee and stewed.

How could he do this to me? To us?

We could pose and pretend in front of the cameras, but that was a private moment. That was real.

At least, I thought it was.

Had it just been a publicity stunt for him? I really hoped not. I don't think we could recover from that. I could forgive a lot, but that was a line we couldn't cross.

"Where's Noah?"

"Did you two fight?"

"Is the engagement over?"

I stared at my cup, trying to block them out.

I was almost finished with my drink when the questions began again. "Noah, where have you been?"

"Are you two engaged?"

"Is she pregnant, Noah?"

Ugh, would they drop that one?

I looked up and watched him come toward me. I looked at the frozen pond and ignored his approach.

"Colby. I'm so sorry." I ignored him, and he sat next to me. "You have to believe me. I didn't tell anyone what happened. Someone must have been listening."

That's what I wanted to think too, but I knew better.

"Stop it, Noah. There's no one else who could have heard. We were alone on the dance floor."

"People can read lips. They could have had a mic on me."

I stopped him.

"You expect me to believe someone wired you?"

The paparazzi were still yelling out questions but were standing far enough away to let us talk.

"I don't know, Colby. I've been wracking my brain since Bryce called me. I have no idea how they found out."

"Bryce called you?" I finally met his eyes.

"Yeah, he told me good job. I didn't understand until he told me about the news that was spreading. He told me we're on all the tabloids. Some are saying we're getting married. Some say we broke up and got back together last night."

"How did they find out?"

He shook his head. "I have no idea, Colby. It could have been someone working the event. Maybe a reporter was there. I don't know, but I swear to you it wasn't me. I wouldn't share our moments with the world."

I felt a little better knowing that. I trusted him. I did.

Maybe I let my fear get the best of me. I should have stopped and really thought about it. Or talked to him. We really needed to communicate better.

"I don't want to be mad at you."

He smiled. "Then don't be."

I slid next to him and put my arms around his waist. "How did you find me?"

"Well, I came back from getting breakfast and you were gone. I ran down to the café and they told me you'd been there but left. They said you were being followed and they thought they saw you come here."

"It's a big park, how did you know I'd be here?"

He kissed my forehead. "It's our spot. It's where I would have gone."

I smiled at that. I might not have planned on coming here, but my feet brought me. Maybe my body knew exactly where I needed to be.

"I'm sorry. I shouldn't have accused you of that."

He pulled me in tighter. "I would have thought the same thing if I was in your position. I'm just glad you forgive me."

I looked up and met his eyes. "There's nothing to forgive."

He kissed me lightly before pulling back. "Are you hungry? I have breakfast waiting for us."

I nodded and stood. "Yes, please."

25

NOAH

I reheated the breakfast burritos I'd gotten us and set them in front of our spots at the bar.

"Thanks, Noah."

I nodded. She wasn't the same. There was something still wrong. We ate in silence while I tried to figure out how to get it out of her.

When she was done, she sighed and started pulling the remaining tortilla into tiny pieces.

"What is it, Colby?"

She looked at me and dropped the tortilla. "I'm freaking out a little bit."

"About what?"

She shrugged, but I wasn't letting her off the hook that easily. I knew something was going on. I just needed her to talk to me.

"What is it?"

She was silent for a moment. "I'm scared."

Her voice was barely a whisper. I would have missed what she said if I wasn't watching her. "Of what?"

She shrugged again, and I realized I was going to have to pull this from her. "Please talk to me, Colby."

She looked at me with watery eyes. "I'm scared of us."

I narrowed my eyes. "Us? What does that mean?"

"What if we don't work? What if we mess up what we have?"

I shook my head. "Colby, we spend almost all of our time together. You know me better than anyone. I like to think I know you, too. We are basically a couple. Now it's just official...to us. Why does that scare you?"

"What if it doesn't last?"

"You can't think like that. You can't doom us from the beginning. We're going to try and we're going to be amazing together. In a week, you'll wonder why you ever doubted."

She tried to smile, but it didn't quite reach her eyes. "There's so much at stake. You're not going to want to work with me if we break up. I should find someone to replace me."

I put my arms on her shoulders and turned her toward me. "What? No. I swear to you. I will not let this affect our professional relationship." A tear rolled down her cheek. "Colby, I care so much about you. I promise to take care of you. I promise to do everything in my power to never hurt you."

She sniffed, and it broke my heart. I never wanted to be the cause of her pain.

"Okay."

"Okay? You trust me?"

"I have to."

I nodded. "You do. I'm not really giving you any other option."

She smiled. "Nope."

"I've got to get ready for practice. Are you coming?"

She nodded. "I'll be there."

"Great."

I kissed the top of her head and hurried to my room. I had an idea, but I was going to need the help of some of the guys.

I texted the team and asked for anyone that could, to get to practice early. Then I showered and changed.

"I'll see you later."

"Bye. Be safe."

I kissed her quickly before grabbing my bag and walking out.

When I got to the locker room Erik, Hartman, Brassard, Reese, Olli, and Porter were all waiting.

"What's going on, Malkin?"

I looked at Hartman and rubbed my hands on my sides. I was nervous, but I knew this would work.

"I need your help. It's not going to be easy, but it will be worth it. To me."

They all looked at each other then back at me.

"What is it?" Erik looked skeptical.

"How well do you guys know the song, 'I just called to say I love you?'"

They all groaned, but Reese laughed. "Oh man. What are you going to do to us?"

I told them my plan and to my complete astonishment they agreed. We went out to the ice and practiced before everyone else got there. When Coach Rust got there, I pulled him to the side and told him my plan. He wasn't exactly happy I chose to interrupt practice, but he didn't tell me no.

"Thanks, Coach."

He shook his head and waved me off. I was getting nervous as women from the Pride began to fill in. I didn't see

Colby though. Had something come up? Was she not coming anymore?

She had to. I wouldn't freak out until practice started.

I did a few laps, racing Reese, before gathering with the team in front of Coach Romney.

When he dismissed us to run drills I glanced at the section where the Pride was. There she was.

She waved, and I smiled and waved back.

Yes.

I tried to focus. I really did, but my mind was on what was coming. Luckily, we didn't have that many people watching us today. I don't know if I could go through it with the general manager watching.

When Rust blew the whistle, the music changed. My song came on and a few of the guys looked around. They were probably confused. Stevie Wonder wasn't exactly on our normal mix.

I skated to the center of the ice and began the steps we practiced. Next, Erik joined in, then Reese, Olli, Hartman, and Brassard. By the time we got to the chorus the rest of the team was laughing hysterically and the Pride was hovered around Colby. They knew what this was. My eyes didn't leave hers as I skated closer to the glass in front of her. I sang out the words.

"I just called to say I love you."

Her mouth dropped, and her cheeks were flushed.

The music ended, and I waited for her reaction. Everyone was watching us. I could feel it. Do something Colby. Anything.

Emma nudged her, and Colby smiled. She stood and put her hand on the glass. I put mine up against hers. "I love you."

I shouted it even though I knew she could hear me if I spoke normally.

"I love you, too."

Everyone started cheering and I saw a tear fall from her eye. I shook my head. That wasn't what I wanted. I never wanted to make her cry. She wiped it and started laughing.

Good. She was happy. Those were happy tears.

A whistle blew behind me and Coach Romney was waving his hand. "Alright, that's enough lovey dovey stuff for today. Get back to work."

I looked back at Colby and she blew me a kiss. I waved and went back to the drills.

The rest of practice flew by. I knew Coach was pushing us hard for my little interruption, and when he finally called it I was dead on my feet.

I followed the guys into the tunnel and was slammed into the wall by a body.

"I can't believe you did that." Colby's face was flushed.

I wrapped my arms around Colby. "Were you surprised?"

"Completely. How did you pull it off?"

"I got them to come to practice early and we put it together. Turns out Hartman has moves."

She laughed, and her smile could have lit up the room. "You made me so happy."

"You make me happy. I'm sorry I acted like an idiot. I promise I'll work on having more of a balance."

"Good."

"Malkin. In my office. Now." I cringed at Coach's voice. He did not sound happy.

"I've got to go."

"Good luck." She leaned forward and kissed me briefly. It was enough to make the worry disappear. Coach could tell me anything. He could yell at me until his voice went hoarse and I wouldn't care.

I went into his office where he was waiting for me. "Take a seat."

I did and waited. I knew from experience with my parents to never speak first. They'll get you to admit to something. Nope. I wasn't digging my own grave.

"Aside from the little charade you pulled today, you've been excellent lately. I'm really proud of how far you've come."

I nodded. "Thank you, sir."

"I know you've been working hard, and you really blew me away at the last game."

I was shocked. Coach didn't seem like the type to give compliments freely.

"I'm not the only one who's noticed."

I sat up. Was this it? Was he going to tell me the decision?

"The office has been impressed as well." He opened and drawer and pulled out a folder. He opened it and slid it over to me.

"They want you, as do I and the rest of the team, to officially join the Fury."

I let out the breath I'd been holding. I couldn't believe it. I'd done it.

"Thank you, Coach."

He cracked a smile. "You did this. You deserve it."

I shook my head. This had been my dream since I could first skate. I wanted this so bad and now it was my reality.

"Take it home and look it over. Have your agent read over it. Sign it when you're ready and bring it back."

I closed the folder and stood. I knew it wouldn't matter. I would take any amount they offered for any length of time.

None of that mattered. I was going to stay, and I was going to be with Colby.

I opened the door to a full hall. Colby rushed forward followed by Erik, Reese, Chloe, Madi, Hartman, and Brassard.

"What did he say?" Colby asked with as much excitement as me.

"Are you fired?" Erik asked with a laugh. Madi punched him and turned to face me.

I slowly held up the folder. "I got a contract!"

Everyone started cheering. Colby wrapped her arms around me and everyone else joined in a massive group hug. This was real. This was my team.

"I'm so proud of you." Colby kissed my cheek.

"Me too." Reese kissed my other cheek which caused a train reaction. Everyone tried to plant one on me. I tried to dodge them but there were too many.

"Welcome to the fury, Malkin." Hartman was the last to get me.

"Thanks guys."

"I knew you could do it."

I looked down at Colby. "Thank you."

"I love you." She smiled, and I couldn't help but mimic her.

"I love you too."

Thanks for reading! I hope you enjoyed Noah and Colby's story!
Word of mouth is so important for authors to succeed. If you enjoyed Match Penalty, I'd love for you to leave a review on Amazon!

Keep Reading,
Xoxo B

Coming in November:
Wyatt and Kendall's Story

He's the captain of the Utah Fury, and she's the number one fan of their rivals. Can their attraction overcome their differences?
To be notified when this book is released join Brittney's Reader List.

Keep reading for a sneak peek into their story.

WYATT

I stepped out my building pulling my cap lower over my eyes with my left hand, strategically blocking my face from the cameras. Even with my lame excuse for a disguise, it was hard to cover up the fact I was over six foot and a bit more muscular than the average person.

I walked down the sidewalk with purpose, I checked in the windows of the shops I passed but didn't see anyone following me. Had they really missed me?

Huh. Maybe moving had worked.

When I asked Chloe and Colby for recommendations on where to live, they both said the same building as Noah Malkin. It was close to the arena and within walking distance of plenty of restaurants and cafes.

It was fine with me. My address had gotten out to too many reporters, and even the public. The guys helped me move in at night, so no one saw.

The reporters and paparazzi at this building were on the lookout for Noah and Colby, so I was able to hide in plain sight. They were one of the most famous couples right now, at least in the sports world. Noah was the top rookie in the league and people loved them together.

Their notoriety was a blessing for me. It'd been almost a month since I moved in, and still no one outside of the team knew where I was. It was glorious. I had more freedom than I'd ever had since joining the NHL almost ten years ago.

I checked over my shoulder one more time before walking into the café Noah had introduced me to. He said no one had ever bothered him and the other customers ignored him. It sounded perfect the first time he told me about it, and now it was a part of my routine. I came every morning that I could.

I had a regular drink, a regular seat, and a regular barista.

It was predictable. Reliable. My one source of normalcy in my crazy life.

I got in line and waited. I didn't check my phone or look at the TVs. This was my place of peace.

When I got to the counter I paused. This was not Matt. Matt was a college student with more piercings than a tattoo parlor and a beanie that had most likely never been washed. I liked Matt. He didn't talk.

I eyed the perky looking blonde in front of me. She looked like she was in her early twenties. Blue eyes. Big smile.

She looked like a fan.

I almost turned and walked out.

"What can I get started for you?"

She had a cup in one hand and marker posed in the other.

"A regular with sugar."

"No cream?"

I shook my head.

238

"Your name?"

Matt didn't ask my name. He didn't even write anything down. We just made eye contact when it was ready, and he gave me a nod.

"Dave."

She nodded and wrote on the cup.

"That will be two-thirty-nine."

I handed her three singles and walked away. I didn't like how attentive she was. She was the type to draw attention. Yell my name so everyone turned and looked. The last thing I wanted was for this place to be exploited.

Maybe the girls from the Pride were right. I should have my assistant do things like this. As nice as it would be, I knew I couldn't. This was one of the few things I did on my own, for myself. My world was the team. Everything I did was somehow related to the team. This, my cup of coffee, was my only place outside of that world. Sure, it would be more convenient. My stress levels would decrease but giving this up would further isolate me from the rest of the world.

Chloe said I needed a hobby.

I told her it was hockey.

Madeline said I needed a girlfriend.

I told her I was planning on being an eternal bachelor.

Colby said I needed a vacation.

I told her I didn't have time.

I didn't have time for model cars or dating. I only had time for workouts, practice, meetings, interviews, charities, galas, events, and whatever else the team needed me to do. Time for myself was a foreign concept.

I'd made my bed, and now I had to lay in it.

Not that I regretted any decision that got me to this point. I was living my dream. I was in a position very few ever experienced. I was in my prime, playing hockey professionally, and on the championship team.

I just wished I could go outside without feeling paranoid. Like someone was going to attack me or rabid fan would maul me for the chance to say they touched my shirt. No thanks.

"Dave."

I looked up to see the blonde smiling wide and holding out my cup. I walked to the counter and took it from her.

"Thanks."

"Have a nice day." She said it a little too sweetly. I eyed her before turning and walking to my normal spot, a leather chair in front of a coffee table packed with old newspapers.

I sat down and closed my eyes for a second. I needed to relax. I was getting paranoid.

Maybe yoga could be my hobby. I bet none of the guys would mock me for that.

What did I care? I was the captain. Actually, I could probably tell Coach it would be good training and make all of them do it with me. That wouldn't be such a bad idea. Every athlete could stand to be more flexible and calm.

I took a sip of my coffee.

Paused.

Lifted the lid up enough for me to promptly spit it out.

What the world?

That was the most disgusting thing I've ever had. I looked to the counter where Blondie was smiling. She didn't even bother looking away. She did this. She ruined my coffee. My one moment of peace. My sanctuary.

I stood and stomped toward her. "What did you do?"

She smiled and shrugged. "I'm not sure what you mean, Dave."

The way she said the name made me suspicious. I

looked around the prep area. You have got to be kidding me. There was a salt shaker next to the sugar.

That little...

"Oh no." Her eyes went big, round and she pouted. "Did I mix up the salt? Oh boy, it's my first day and I'm still getting used to things."

I narrowed my eyes. "You mixed up salt and sugar?"

She batted her eyes at me. "It's an honest mistake, mister."

Alright, she was laying it on a little thick. The whole oh golly me act wasn't working for her.

I tried to keep my voice even. I was ready to yell and scream at her like I would to an opponent on the ice. "Can I ask what I did to deserve this?"

Her eyes narrowed, and her entire demeanor changed. She crossed her arms and sized me up. "Ollisac, game four, that was an illegal hit and you know it."

I stepped back. What was she talking about? Ollisac. The center from the Baltimore Harbors? We'd played them in the finals two years ago.

I couldn't remember what hit she was talking about.

"What are you –"

She took a step closer to me, almost toe to toe. "Cut the crap, Hartman. You know what you did."

I held up my hands and took a step back. "As shocking as it might be I don't remember ever single hit or penalty. I do remember that we beat the Harbors four to oh that series."

She followed me, not backing down. "Because Ollisac was out the rest of the game."

I rolled my eyes. "There's no coming back in game four. They weren't going to come back and sweep the rest of the series."

She looked defiant. "Guess we'll never know since you seem to slide by the refs without ever getting called."

Alright. Now she's just being dramatic. "You and I both know I spend my share of time in the penalty box. Don't act like I'm never sent in."

She folded her arms. "Barely."

I shrugged. "I don't do things to deserve it."

She shook her head. "If only my uncle was here."

"Why so he could get revenge on something that happened two years ago to someone he's never even met?"

I didn't actually know that. She would be Ollisac's cousin for all I knew.

She shook her head. "It doesn't matter. I stay loyal."

I looked around. "So loyal you moved to the heart of the enemy territory?"

Her eyes dropped for just a second. "It's not by choice."

Yeah, I understood not having a say in where you live.

It wasn't an excuse for bad customer service or ruining someone's drink, though. I looked around for Matt, or anyone else I recognized, but it looked like she was alone.

"Where's the manager?"

Her face when blank and she jumped back. "What?"

"The manager? Or Matt?"

She stuttered and seemed to have lost all the fight she'd had moments before. "Uh. Oh. Um. Why?"

I held up my cup. "This is not okay. I don't care if you have some old vendetta against me. I'm a paying customer. I'm a regular here. I want to talk to someone about making sure this won't happen again."

The color in her face drained. Huh. Not so cocky now.

"That won't be necessary. I can assure you it won't happen again."

I raised an eyebrow. "Oh really. You are going to reassure me? The person that did it in the first place?"

"I had to. My uncle would never let it go if I did get some sort of revenge when I had the chance."

I counted to ten to keep from yelling at her.

"That's cute that you and your uncle can have your little joke, but I'm real. I'm not just an athlete on the TV. This is my life. This is my neighborhood. My home. This is the café I come to every day." I paused and looked at her. "Well, maybe not anymore. I'll have to find somewhere else to go."

She looked panicked. "I'm sorry. I shouldn't have done that."

I set down my cup and slid it toward her. "No. You shouldn't have. You're a grown woman, and this is your job. You shouldn't abuse that situation for your own kicks and giggles."

I turned and strode out.

I was so sick of being treated like a character. Like I'm only a hockey player. Something for people to cheer at. Mock. Dissect. Discuss.

I was a person. Someone with a life outside of the arena. I had friends and family and my own issues to deal with.

I just wished people realized that.

The guys on the team were lucky. Olli and Porter got married young, before their status became their identity. Erik, Reese, and Noah found women that really understood their lives and all that came with their profession and what they were getting into. They knew the person, rather than the player.

I doubted I'd ever find that.

Since my relaxation time was cut short, I headed back to my building to grab my bag. Might as well get some alone time in the gym.

I snuck by the cameras again and made it to my apartment without incident. I was in the locker room ten minutes later. I changed and walked into the gym, finding it lit up. I looked around and saw Noah and Brassard at the squat rack.

Not the alone time I'd been looking forward to, but at least it wasn't the whole team.

"Hey guys."

Noah waved but kept his eyes on Brassard who was mid-squat.

I went to a treadmill to warm up and put in my headphones. The peace only lasted one song. The guys were waving me over and I didn't want to seem like a jerk.

I paused my music and walked over. "What are you guys doing here?"

It wasn't surprising to see them together. The two defensemen had formed quite the bond over the last few months of Noah being here. I'd called it a bromance once, but they didn't care.

"Fitting in an extra leg day. What are you doing here?" Noah looked suspicious. He'd already made comments about my routine and tight schedule. I was here when I should be at the café. He thought I was too uptight. I thought he was too young, and spontaneous.

"My morning plans changed." I knew I sounded gruffer than I should have, given it was just a cup of coffee. But it was more than that. It was my place.

"Did something happen?" Noah looked to Brassard who looked back to me.

"I had an encounter with a new barista. You should probably stay away from her, Noah."

Brassard chuckled. "Did she hit on you?"

"No."

"Did she make a scene?" Noah asked.

"No."

"Did she get your order wrong?" Brassard wasn't even trying to hide his smile.

"Sort of."

They both smirked. Noah had to decency to shake it off. "What happened?"

"She put salt in my coffee instead of sugar. When I called her out on it, she told me it was to get back at me from a hit two years ago."

Brassard looked confused. "You hit her?"

"No. I hit Ollisac."

"When?" Noah looked equally perplexed.

"Two years ago. During the finals."

Noah held up a hand. "So, this chick ruined your coffee because of a play, two years ago?"

I nodded. They seemed to finally understand the level of crazy I'd confronted.

"That's messed up." Noah shook his head.

"So, I'm guessing she isn't a Fury fan." Brassard cringed.

"Nope. Baltimore Harbors." I clarified.

Brassard chuckled. "That's a rarity here."

"Yeah, and apparently, she hates us, or at least me."

Noah gasped. "Someone that doesn't fall at the feet of the all mighty Hartman?"

I glared at him. "That's not the point. That café has been compromised."

He smiled. "Don't worry, man. I'll go in with you tomorrow and make sure the big scary lady doesn't mess with your drink."

I considered punching him. I really wanted to.

Coach would probably frown upon that.

Instead of starting a fight, I walked back to the treadmill and turned my music up to block out the noise. Sometimes running was the best option for getting out my frustration. Today, it saved Noah's face.

He could tease me now, but just wait until she got him. He might be new to the team, but he'd already created some upsets. I was sure she wasn't a fan of his either.

ABOUT THE AUTHOR

Brittney has been an avid reader for as long as she can remember. Her parents' form of punishment growing up was taking away her books and making her go outside to play. She loves the beach, exercising, sleeping in, and cookies. Yes, she does know those contradict each other. She's an obsessive dog lover and is slowly learning to appreciate the mountains she lives in. Nature can be okay, sometimes.